I0557442

Rogue's Revenge

by

Gail MacMillan

Rogue's Revenge

Cover Art by *Tina Lynn Stout*

The Wild Rose Press, Inc.
PO Box 708
Adams Basin, NY 14410-0708
Visit us at www.thewildrosepress.com

Publishing History
First Champagne Rose Edition, 2013
Digital ISBN 978-1-61217-791-5
Print ISBN 978-1-62830-097-0

Published in the United States of America

"I've shanghaied you." He put aside his paddle, picked up the canteen, and took a swallow before recapping it.

"Kidnapped, you mean." Outrage surmounted all her previous emotions.

"No, shanghaied." He plunged his paddle deep, sending the canoe to the right to avoid a rock. "You'll be working your passage."

"Oh, I don't think so. And for future reference, what did you do while I was out cold?" she raged.

"Loaded you into a sleeping bag and this canoe." He kept his eyes focused over her head, at the river beyond. "Check your clothes if you're concerned. I've never been turned on by an inebriated woman."

"I was not inebriated, you backstreet slim. Ouch!" Her outburst brought on a pounding ache above her eyes. She caught her head between her hands. "Take me back to the Lodge right now! Otherwise, I'll have you charged with kidnapping!"

"Really? I'm shaking in my boots. You'll feel better after you've had a couple of aspirin and some lunch."

"Don't you dare laugh at me!" She clenched her fists and sucked in her lips. "I'm deadly serious!"

"Well, then, that's too bad. Because I can't take you back. We're a good six miles downriver from the Lodge, deep into roadless wilderness, and with the force of the freshet that's pushing us, a superhero couldn't paddle us back upstream." He dipped his paddle deep and nosed the canoe to the left.

"Hang on," he ordered. "We're heading into rapids."

Praise for Gail MacMillan

"Ms. MacMillan spins a lovely story of romance and suspense. This is a great romance. I can't wait to read her next one."

~Robin, Romancing the Book
~*~

"Really enjoyed this book! Very well written and made me feel I was there, inside the story. Excellent read. I give this book 5 sighs."

~Let's Talk Romance Reviews
~*~

So, what do you get when you mix these two [hero and heroine], a pug, a German Shepherd, a lot of jinx and a mystery? Amazingly good book, that's what! *HOLDING OFF FOR A HERO* is an incredibly entertaining read. The characters are great, the chemistry is there from the start, and even though they are doing their best to ignore it, they will fail miserably. There are a lot of witty moments, and just the way Emma is getting under Frasier's skin, against his will of course, is enough to make this book worth reading….I love this little adventure! It's sweet, but it won't give you a toothache. There's suspense, but it's not overshadowing the romance. There are quite a few surprises along the way. You'll keep guessing what's going on and keep hoping Frasier and Emma will get their happy ending. It's one light, wonderful read I gladly recommend."

~Rain Hart, The Romance Reviews

Dedication

To my faithful canine companions
Molly and Barbie-Q.

Chapter One

Allison and her mother followed the pallbearers and coffin out onto the church steps and she saw him for the first time in over a dozen years. Standing alone in the fog beside the waiting hearse, his field coat and Snowy River hat filmed with mist, he brought memories stabbing like a knife blade back into her heart.

Why did he come? He knew I'd be here. Doesn't he have any shame? Couldn't he leave me in peace today of all days?

The last time she'd seen him he'd been a lanky teenager in faded jeans and black leather jacket, a rude comeback always ready on his lips, a defiant challenge in his tawny eyes.

But during her years of absence he'd filled out. The open jacket didn't hide broad shoulders and a lean, firm torso. Beneath it he wore a faded green shirt, with khaki bush pants below. His boots were scuffed and muddy.

Gramps didn't change him. Heath Oakes is still a hoodlum who doesn't even know how to dress for the funeral of the man who was like a father to him.

When he looked in her direction, Alison knew his attitude toward her hadn't altered, either. The moment he recognized her, his mouth curled into a deprecating smirk. He let the power of his feral gaze roam over her. Then he pulled off his hat and strode up the church

1

steps two at a time to assist the pallbearers struggling to get her grandfather's coffin down the narrow wooden stairway of the century-old country church. Seizing the brass handle on the rear left side, he swung the casket about as easily as Allison recalled he could turn a canoe in the river's current.

"Dad was right," Allison heard her mother breathe. "He said Heath was a man who knew how to take charge."

Myra Armstrong squared her slender shoulders and, with Allison by her side, led the mourners down the church steps behind her father's casket. In her black Italian trench coat and wide-brimmed hat, she was the epitome of quiet elegance. She moved with an easy, self-assured grace that came from years of practice and well-received results. The few tiny lines at the corners of her soft green eyes suggested an age little more than that of Allison's older sister if she'd had one. Once, when Allison and Myra had been visiting a horse-breeding farm in search of a new hunter, Allison had overheard one of the grooms refer to Myra as a classy broad. That said it all.

Allison pulled herself back to the moment and joined her mother as Jack Adams' friends and neighbors surrounded them. One by one they shook hands, offered their condolences, got into their vehicles, and drove out of the mist-shrouded country churchyard. They'd been informed during the funeral service that the graveside ceremony was for family only. Allison, Myra, the undertaker, and Heath were left standing in the thickening fog at the back of the hearse.

"Well." Myra forced a smile. She swept it wide enough to include Heath and the austere man in black,

2

as well as her daughter. "Shall we go? Heath, will you drive with us?"

"Thanks, Mrs. Armstrong, but I have my own vehicle." He jerked a thumb in the direction of a battered old canvas-topped Jeep parked a short distance off in the mist. "I'll meet you there."

He slapped his hat back over the dark blond hair that curled below his ears and shot Allison another critical head-to-toe appraisal.

You can't make me squirm, you bit of back-street trash. You won't.

She stuck out her chin and faced him with what she hoped was an appearance of absolute disdain.

But as their gazes met, her resolve faltered. Why had he grown up to be such eye candy? Why couldn't he have been as ugly as his parting shot at her all those years ago? The rugged outdoorsman face, bronzed by sun and wind, had the firm jaw lines, high cheekbones, and intense untamed eyes that could easily send a woman's pulse racing to triple speed.

On occasion, it must have. Allison remembered one of her mother's wealthy friends describing her visit to her grandfather's wilderness lodge and nature retreat, the Chance, where Heath was guide foreman and camp manager.

"Robert fished," Candace Breckenridge had drawled as she sat draped over a chaise longue at the Armstrong's Muskoka summer place, "while I found my pleasure with that decidedly delicious and heroic-looking wild-woodsman-type guide named Heath. Lord, even his name is earthy and wild! The minute I laid eyes on him, I knew I had to have him. Myra, tell your father never, never to fire that magnificent

3

creature. And that ridiculous scare I had added just the right amount of seasoning to the whole adventure."

"What scare?" Myra asked.

"Oh, come on now, Myra. You know. Almost being caught? The intrigue is half the fun. But enough in front of the child." She waved toward Allison.

Allison had stifled the urge to scoff. Magnificent creature? That skinny kid with the rotten manners charming a sophisticated woman like Candace Breckenridge? Preposterous! Now, as she looked at him, she mentally revised her opinion of the possibility.

Her thoughts were interrupted by the arrival of a Lincoln Continental. The big black car bumped up the dirt road into the churchyard and lurched to a stop close to the hearse. Its driver stepped out, a middle-aged man of medium height, his iron-gray hair, well-tailored charcoal business suit, pearl-white shirt, and silk tie presenting an impeccable appearance.

"Mrs. Armstrong?" He strode over to Myra. "James Wilcox, ma'am, National Realty. Allow me to express my sincere condolences on your loss."

He would have been a handsome man if it hadn't been for something hard and measuring in his expression. Smooth, calculating, probably ruthless. As CFO of one of Canada's leading corporations, Allison had no trouble recognizing the signs.

"And this must be your lovely daughter." He turned to Allison. "First woman to crack the higher echelons of the Shawville Corporation. Quite an accomplishment, young lady, but being the child of one of Canada's leading neurosurgeons must have helped."

Anger shot through her. She'd worked seventy-hour weeks. She'd denied herself a social life. How dare he imply—

"Thank you." Myra shot Allison a silencing glance. "Have we met?"

"No." The smile that tilted the corners of his mouth didn't reach sapphire-cold blue eyes. "But I had approached your father with an offer to purchase his holdings shortly before…the tragedy. I still have a client prepared to make a handsome offer for his lodge and grounds."

"Buy the Chance?" Myra's astonishment rang in her voice. "I…really, I'm not…this is hardly an appropriate moment to discuss…"

"Mrs. Armstrong doesn't want to talk business." Heath stepped between her mother and the stranger. "I suggest you leave…now."

"I'd prefer to hear that decision from the lady herself." James Wilcox held his ground.

"Shove off, Wilcox. Jack wouldn't do business with you, and neither will his daughter."

"Mrs. Armstrong, are you going to let this backwoods hoodlum turn away an excellent offer—"

"Please." Myra held up a hand and lowered her head, shaking it in weary confusion.

Heath's hands shot out and grabbed James Wilcox's lapels. So fast it made Allison gasp, he dragged the man to his car and stuffed him inside.

"You can't do this!" Wilcox yelled, but the door slammed on his words. He shook a fist and yelled muffled threats through the glass. Heath turned and walked back to the group at the hearse.

"You haven't heard the last of this, Oakes!" The man lowered the window and shouted. "I'll be back." Tearing up the church yard lawn, the big car whirled and headed off into the fog.

"Thank you, Heath. I can't bear to discuss disposing of Dad's property, especially not today."

"No problem. We'd better get started."

He turned away into the mist. Allison watched as he climbed into the dilapidated Jeep he'd indicated earlier and revved the motor.

"Come on, darling." Myra took her daughter by the elbow to urge her toward their rental car. "We'll meet Heath at the lane, Mr. Jenkins," she informed the undertaker, "just as soon as we pick up our luggage at the motel."

"Are you sure you can manage, Mrs. Armstrong?" The tall, thin man furrowed his pale forehead and rubbed gloved hands together. "I've taken care of every detail that I possibly can, but this is a highly unusual arrangement."

"You've covered all the legalities, Mr. Jenkins. Heath can manage the rest."

"Mom, what do you mean, 'all the legalities, Heath can manage the rest'?" Allison hissed as mother and daughter started toward their car. "What haven't you told me? Gramps is going to be buried in the church cemetery, isn't he?"

"No, dear, he isn't." Myra paused, a slender black-gloved hand on the handle of the driver's door, and turned to look at her daughter. "He's going to be buried at Adam's Landing. It was his last wish. I've secured the legal clearances."

"Mom, no! That canoe landing is in the middle of nowhere. It's only accessible by the river route. This is crazy, especially at this time of year, with a full freshet flooding down from the mountains!" Allison couldn't believe what she was hearing.

"Actually, there is a land route." Her mother slid behind the wheel. "It's rough, but Heath has assured me we can manage."

"We…three…alone?" This had to be some crazy, surreal dream full of dense spring fog and crazy ideas…

"Get in, dear." Her mother started the motor. "It looks like rain. The trail out to the Landing isn't the best even on a dry summer's day, and we still have to pick up our suitcases at the motel before checkout time. We mustn't keep Heath waiting."

The whole world has gone nuts, and it's dragging me along with it. She got into the passenger seat.

"Mom, that man, James Wilcox." *I have to get a handle on reality. Discuss something down to earth and sane…like business.* "Maybe you should at least hear what he has to say. Not now," she hastened as Myra threw her an exasperated glance. "But later, after the will is read. You'll be looking to sell the place and…"

"Allison, really! Your grandfather is barely gone, and you're discussing liquidation of his assets." She shifted into drive, and headed the car out of the churchyard.

"Mom, I…"

"Enough. I don't want us to quarrel today of all days. We have to concentrate on carrying out your grandfather's last wishes."

She glanced over at her daughter, whose tears brimmed as she shook her head and replied, "I'm sorry. It's just that everything about today is turning out all wrong."

"You mean Heath." Myra blinked and focused her attention on the road.

"Don't be ridiculous, Mom. As if I cared about a piece of street trash Gramps rescued simply to get his mother as housekeeper after Gram died. He should have found some other lady for the job and left Heath Oakes where he belongs…in prison."

"I don't know what the man did to inspire you with such hatred, but just for today let's leave the past alone and focus on the chore ahead." Her mother's words brooked no room for further discussion.

Forty-five minutes later, Myra pulled the car onto the shoulder of the narrow country road. Headed down a rutted, impassable-looking trail that led into the bush on the right was a dirty, dented relic that must once have been a farm tractor. Jack Adams' coffin lay strapped to the wooden trailer hitched to it. Heath Oakes glanced up from checking the straps that held it in place and touched his hat brim in Myra's direction. The undertaker was not present.

"Mom, this is insane." Allison whirled on her mother. "You can't believe the three of us are going to take Gramps' remains down this road with that…thing and bury his coffin?"

"Allison." Myra placed a hand on her daughter's shoulder. "This was his last wish. It's the least I can do. I wasn't exactly the best of daughters."

"He never believed that for a minute." Allison couldn't bear the remorse in her mother's voice and expression. "He loved you. He never blamed you for marrying Dad and moving away."

"And how often did I visit him?" Myra jerked the key from the ignition. "I was so busy with my family and with fundraising, I rarely visited him. Even after your grandmother died, even when I should have

8

known how lost and lonely he must have been without her. If it hadn't been for Heath and Ella Oakes…"

"He did *them* the kindness!" *How could a clever woman like her mother be so blind to the reality of the situation!* "Ella Oakes was a destitute widow with no job, no place to live, and a convicted criminal for a son when Gramps took her in. Who else would have done that? And let's not forget her jailbird offspring was alone with Gramps when he died…"

"That's quite enough!" Myra Armstrong met her daughter's blazing green-eyed defiance with an unfaltering emerald one. "Heath and his mother saved your grandfather from loneliness and despair after your grandmother died. They did what you and I, his daughter and granddaughter, should have done. Don't make any more ridiculous innuendoes. Go tell Heath we'll be with him directly. I want to change my footwear."

"But, Mom…"

"Go."

Allison heaved an exasperated sigh and climbed out of the car. The Oakes had completely finessed Myra Armstrong.

The wet chip-sealed road made walking in high heels a balancing act. By the time she reached Heath, her temper hadn't improved.

"My mother's coming," she muttered. "She's changing her shoes."

"Wouldn't hurt you to do the same." He paused in checking the straps and glanced down at her black pumps. "You and your mother will have to walk. There's no room for passengers."

"I don't have anything even remotely suitable for

trekking through the sea of mud that trail appears to be. I had no idea we'd be indulging in this kind of expedition when we left Toronto."

"There's a pair of rubber boots in the back of my Jeep." He gave the restraints another jerk. "They'll be a bit big, but they'll be better than those things you're wearing."

The sharp retort brewing in her throat died as her mother came striding up to them, feet encased in Wellingtons.

"Ready?" Myra drew a deep breath and pulled back her shoulders.

"As soon as Ms. Armstrong gets herself appropriately shod." He looked down at the older woman, his tone and outlook softening.

"Oh, darling, I forgot to tell you to bring boots." Her mother stared down at her daughter's feet.

"I've told her I have boots in the back of my Jeep she can borrow." He gave the coffin a light slap, as if he were patting the man inside on the back. A corner of his mouth twitched in a grin. "Remembering the good times," he said softly.

Good God, the man can put on an act. If I didn't know him so well, I'd think he was sincere.

"Well, then." Myra turned to her daughter with a what-are-you-waiting-for look. "Get those boots."

Allison shot Heath Oakes what she hoped was a withering look before she swung away and tottered off toward the Jeep. Her attempt at hauteur failed as one of her heels caught in the loose rocks and she had to scramble to keep her balance.

She imagined him smirking behind her back. She'd be glad when all this was over, the will had been read, and her mother, who would inherit her father's holdings, could send him packing.

Pulling a pair of mud-spattered rubber boots—at a glance, several sizes too large—from the Jeep's cluttered cargo space, she jerked off her pumps, and flung the shoes that had cost her several hundred dollars into the back of the dirty vehicle.

I'll convince Mom to dismiss him, come hell or high water, the minute she's in possession of the Chance. We'll see how cocky he is when he's out on his backside!

With the boots flopping a couple of inches from her heels, she stomped back to the tractor and the waiting couple. She caught a glint of wicked amusement flickering in Heath's golden brown eyes. Prickling annoyance flooded through her veins. A black, short-skirted, designer-original suit did not coordinate with filthy, gargantuan Wellingtons.

"Are you ready, Heath?" Myra looked up at the man on the tractor.

"Ready when you are, Mrs. Armstrong."

"Then let's away."

"Yes, ma'am."

He leaned forward and turned a switch. The motor sputtered, then roared to life. He flashed a triumphant grin down on Myra. Focusing his attention on the trail ahead, he put his hand over the gearshift and forced it into drive. All but unseating its driver, the old tractor leaped forward.

"Ride 'em, cowboy," Allison sniggered.

"Allison, really!" Her mother's rebuke reminded her of the solemnity of the occasion.

"Sorry. I couldn't resist."

Heedless of her taunt, Heath got the vehicle under control. As it began to jolt its way down the trail, he settled it into a slow plod through the ruts of spring-softened ground. Myra and Allison fell in behind it, skirting the wake when possible, walking gingerly through the mud when it wasn't.

The mile-long trek to the burial site seemed interminable. Rankled to the core, Allison trudged along beside her apparently undaunted mother. Twice the cloying mud brought her up short and she would have fallen except for Myra's hand grasping her arm.

"Mom, I can't believe Gramps expected us to do this," she muttered. "This trail is awful."

"Heath's managing, darling." Myra paused to indicate the tractor and trailer slogging and lurching down the trail ahead of them. "And so am I. Gramps would have expected you to have appropriate footwear…and a bit of perseverance."

"Mom…" Allison started to protest, but her mother had set off again, following the dirty, roaring vehicle, head held high in her wide-brimmed hat, spatters of mud on the Italian leather coat that looked entirely out of place above filthy farm boots. Her mother was one amazing woman. She shook her head and followed.

A half hour later they emerged into a meadow carpeted with the dry, dead grasses left over from winter. In the mist, it was a dull brown expanse surrounded by walls of dark brooding spruce and solemn white pine. Somewhere several yards ahead, obscured by the fog, the river thundered past, swollen with the freshet of melting mountain snows. Allison visualized its dangerous, swollen torrent. She remembered another springtime years earlier, when a

12

gangly teenage boy had dared her to canoe its length with him. His challenge had earned her the only dressing down she could ever recall getting from her grandfather.

The tractor's revving and roaring brought her back to the moment. Allison saw Heath backing its trailer up to a freshly dug grave beside a stone monument. She heaved a sigh. *Soon, soon this will be over, and we'll be on our way back to Toronto.*

He parked with the back of the trailer at the lip of the yawning hole, cut the motor, and climbed down as Myra joined him.

"We made it." Her mother put a hand on his arm. "Thank you, Heath."

"Thanks aren't necessary, Mrs. Armstrong," he said. "Are you ready?"

"Definitely. Allison, come over here, please."

While the two women stood side by side next to the trailer, Heath released the restraining straps, pulled out a pin to allow the trailer to tilt, and let the coffin slide into the grave. It stopped with a dull bump.

A sharp sob escaped Myra Armstrong, but she waved away Allison's attempt to put an arm around her. Allison backed off and waited. She knew she'd forever remember the image of her mother, dressed in black, standing beside the open grave, head bent, eyes closed.

Heath, who'd been standing to one side, reached for a shovel stuck in the mound of earth beside the grave.

"Wait…please. I want to say a few words before you…" Allison's heart ached at her mother's request.

He nodded and stepped back.

"Come, Allison." Holding out a hand, Myra

Armstrong moved to stand on the brink of the grave. She paused and closed her eyes. Allison saw tears trickle from beneath the closed lids and slide down her mother's cheeks.

"Join us, Heath," she startled Allison by requesting as she held out her other hand.

"Yes, ma'am." Heath pulled off his hat.

"Let us pray." Holding both their hands, she bowed her head. "Dear Lord, please welcome Jack Adams as he welcomed all those who came to his door. Give him a place in eternity as beautiful as this land he loved, and let him share it with the woman who was his best friend and soul mate. Amen."

"Amen." Heath's voice edging on a croak outraged Allison. *Damn, he's good at pretending he really gives a rat's behind!*

"Dad," Myra startled her daughter by continuing while she held their hands. "Your wishes will be carried out. I'll see to it. Rest in peace."

As if in answer, a robin in a nearby burgeoning birch tree burst into song.

She released their hands and nodded to Heath. "You can begin."

He pulled off his coat and was about to drop it to the ground with his hat, but Myra reached out to take them.

"Thanks," he said. Their gazes met. Allison saw an empathy flash between them. *What is going on here?*

Heath pulled the shovel from the pile of earth beside the grave. The harsh sound of the first clump of dirt hitting the coffin in the misty hush of the meadow cracked the restraint she'd been mastering all day. He was really gone.

"Gramps," she whispered. "Oh, Grampie."

"Come along, darling." Myra put her arm around her shoulders. "We'll take a walk down to the river and let Heath do his work."

Allison paused a moment to look at the man shoveling earth into the grave, feet braced, lean muscular body moving mechanically, easily, it appeared, through the heavy task. His lips were hard set in a grim line, a tick worked in his jaw.

Two-faced bum, putting on an act for my mother. Well, he's not fooling me.

She started around the excavation toward the river. At the granite monument, she stopped.

"Maud Adams. Grandma. I didn't know she was buried here."

"She died in December of that year, you'll remember." Myra touched the stone. "You, your Dad, and I came for the funeral. The ground was frozen, so burial had to be delayed until spring. When the time arrived, your father had several serious cases he couldn't leave, and you were deep in some kind of business merger. I came down alone. After cutting through mountains of red tape, Dad and Ethan Jarvis, the undertaker, had arranged for it to be here. At that time your grandfather had the monument erected and arrangements made to be placed beside her when his time came. Now come along," she urged as Allison felt her eyes fill with tears. "Gramps hated crying women. He never knew what to do with them."

Allison followed her mother away from the gravesites and across the sloping field. When they reached the river, they paused. The torrent thundering past reminded Allison of her tall, barrel-chested grandfather with his thick mane of white hair and booming laugh. He'd had a wonderful tenor voice and often entertained his guests at the Lodge from a repertoire that included everything from show tunes to country-western. Allison had especially enjoyed the times he'd sung "Annie's Song" to her grandmother, who often accompanied him on her acoustic guitar.

What a pair they'd been. Until Gram had been diagnosed with cancer and died slowly before Jack Adams' helpless, desperate eyes.

He'd never sung again. He'd remained jovial with his guests, always appeared happy when he visited Allison and her parents in Ottawa, but he'd never again radiated the overwhelming *joie de vivre* that had once been a nimbus around him.

Was that what love meant? A song bursting in your heart when you had it and silence when it was gone? She'd never know. Her heart had been turned to stone years ago by the man shoveling earth into her grandfather's grave.

"You're cold." Myra put an arm about her daughter and hugged her to her side. "Heath must be finished. We can head back. Dad wouldn't want any of us to catch pneumonia."

"I would have dressed more appropriately if you'd told me these plans." Cold and tiredness brought testiness into Allison's tone.

"I was afraid you'd protest and, frankly, my darling, in the past day and a half since Dad died, I wouldn't have had the strength to argue with you. Especially since your father had several critically ill patients and couldn't come with us. Gramps would have understood his not attending the funeral under those conditions, but you know how I rely on your father's strength at times like this. I need you to be with me, physically and emotionally."

Exhaustion settled over Myra Armstrong's delicately featured face.

"Ignore my whining. I loved Gramps." She gave her mother a quick hug. "I'm willing to do whatever he wanted."

"Are you?" Her mother's green eyes looked into hers, searching deep. "Are you really, Allison? You do know why your grandfather named his lodge and wilderness retreat the Chance, don't you? He thought of it as a place that gave people a chance to find themselves, to discover who and what they really are."

"Of course, but what…?"

"Ready to leave, ladies?" Heath climbed back into the driver's seat. "This time you can ride on the trailer, if you think you can hang on."

"We'll definitely give it a try." Myra headed for the decrepit conveyance. "My feet are killing me, and I'm sure Allison's are in much worse condition."

Chapter Two

"Let's go." Allison's teeth chattered as she huddled against the car, hugging her body while Myra searched her pocket for the key. The black designer suit was poor protection from the cold mist. "Hurry, Mom, hurry. We have to catch that flight back home."

"Oh, didn't I tell you?" Her mother paused with her hand on the door and looked out at her daughter from beneath the brim of her hat. "You'll be staying at Chance Lodge. I have to go back immediately—the fundraising drive for the new children's wing at the hospital is at a crucial point—but a family member has to be here for the reading of the will."

"Me? Stay, at the Lodge—with him?" Allison was sputtering. "No way! I have to get back. My job…"

"Darling, the Shawville Corporation won't go belly-up simply because you're absent another day or two. Get your suitcase out of the trunk and go with Heath." She glanced over her daughter's shoulder and smiled at the man waiting beside the mud-spattered Jeep.

"If you'll give me your key, I'll get your daughter's luggage, Mrs. Armstrong." He strode forward.

"All right, all right." Allison threw up her hands. *Taking charge, bullying his way into their lives. Damn the man!* "But as soon as the lawyer reads that will, I'll be on the next plane to T-O. Agreed?"

"Agreed." Myra handed the key to Heath. As he went to the rear of the car, she embraced her disgruntled daughter. "Thanks, sweetie."

"I'm not sure how Paul will feel about this arrangement, but safe journey, Mom." Allison softened at her mother's imminent departure.

"There you go. You're doing better already. Take care of my girl, Heath," Myra continued to the man who had returned, Allison's oversized suitcase in his hand. "And be forewarned. She recently passed self-defense training with flying colors."

"Noted." He handed her the car key. "Safe journey, Mrs. Armstrong."

"Thank you." She slid into her car, waved, and drove off, windshield wipers battling the thickening mist.

"Who's Paul?" he asked as they watched her out of sight.

"Paul Bradley, my sort-of significant other."

"Sort of? Sounds serious."

She turned on him and recognized disdain in his expression.

"Don't!" she snapped.

"Don't what?"

"Mock me. And don't think you can take advantage of me now that my mother is gone."

"Right." Sarcasm colored the word. "Let's go." He headed for his Jeep.

"What about the tractor?" she asked as she stumbled along behind him in his too-large boots.

"The farmer I borrowed it from will pick it up later today. It's safe. Who'd want to steal the thing?"

For the first time she caught a glimmer of humor in his golden-brown eyes. A smile struggled against her taut lips as they looked at the mud-spattered vehicle and homemade trailer, both scrap-yard ready.

"It did the job." She followed him to the Jeep and flinched as he flung her suitcase into the back. Apparently Italian craftsmanship meant nothing to him.

"Sure did. Jack would have gotten a whale of a belly laugh out of it."

He strode to the driver's side and swung into the seat. Allison slogged around to the passenger side, started to get in, and found herself hobbled by her fitted skirt. No way was it going to allow her to climb into the Jeep without hiking it up higher than she had any intention of doing in his presence.

"What?" he asked, looking over at her as he leaned forward to put the key in the ignition.

"This thing wasn't built with my skirt in mind."

"Argh!" He swung out and strode around to her side of the vehicle. Before she could protest, he'd swept her up into his arms.

A shock shot through her as her knees fell over his arm and she felt her back cradled against his shoulder. A murmur of some brand of masculine soap whispered over her senses. The strength beneath her was astounding. His powerful, easy confidence not only astonished her, it made her heart flip.

He paused to look down at her, and the expression in his tawny eyes melted her like snow in a heat wave. Butterflies sprang to life in her solar plexus, and a shock of something hot and magic shot through her body. Handsome, strong, utterly self-assured in a dangerous, untamed way, the man captivated her physically even as her mind fought to reject him. She now understood Candace Breckenridge's "delicious" and "wild-woods-hero" adjectives. As she looked up into the ruggedly handsome face, her lips parted.

"No." His response crashed over her like a bucket of ice water as he swung her into the Jeep and plunked her down in the passenger seat. *Damn and double damn. He guessed what I was feeling, what he did to me. And worst of all, I'm blushing.*

He strode back to the driver's side and swung into place.

"What do you mean, 'no'?" Allison avoided looking at him as she snapped the dirty belt into place across her damp suit jacket. "Surely you can't be vain enough to think…"

"Look, Ms. Armstrong, I've been propositioned by enough rich city women over the years to recognize a 'take me' invitation when I see one." He leaned forward to turn the key in the ignition, annoyance in his words and tense body movements.

As the engine roared into action, he gathered up his own seatbelt and snapped it into place. He glanced over at her, contempt flashing from eyes fierce with anger as he shifted into drive.

Allison glared a death threat in his direction as the old vehicle lurched to life. She'd never been so insulted in her life. He may have discovered soap and deodorant, but his manners were still those of a hoodlum fresh out of a concrete jungle. How could he possibly imagine that she, Allison Armstrong, daughter of one of Canada's leading neurosurgeons and CFO of a major Canadian corporation, would be interested in him? She worked out at her Toronto gym three mornings a week. His wasn't the first hard body she'd seen.

But it was the earthiest, the most naturally virile, an annoying thought nagged.

She glanced over at him. He did personify a romantic savage, with just the right amount of polish to be a female fantasy come to life, a genuine thrill for the neglected wives of wealthy men.

A vision of Heath with Candace Breckenridge flashed across her mind. *Damn.* She flicked it away like an unacceptable TV channel. Fixing her gaze on the road ahead, she remained silent.

A half hour later when they turned into the lane that led to the Lodge, a gasp escaped her lips. Although it had been years since Allison had visited her grandfather's wilderness retreat, the joy and sense of expectation she'd always experienced on returning resurfaced in a flash.

Over two miles long, the private road was a tunnel hewn out of the branches of an ancient forest of birch, pine, spruce, cedar, and maple. Jack Adams had believed in destroying as little of the natural environment as possible. When he'd established the Lodge, over forty years earlier, he'd uprooted as few trees as possible in making a road to the river. The rest he'd left to grow into a living canopy.

In the mist, diamond-like droplets decorated the needles and awakening leaves that formed this living tunnel. Every tree and shrub glistened in soft green expectation of a new beginning. The air held the fresh rain scent only a place far from pollution can offer.

It's like entering an enchanted forest. I remember thinking you could find every living shade of green here.

When a doe and her spotted fawn appeared in front of them, their beauty made her breath catch in her throat. The doe's alert body was a reddish amber, she and her spotted, wide-eyed baby the epitome of pristine innocence.

Heath eased to a stop and turned off the motor.

"They're gorgeous!" Allison breathed.

"Just a bit of what your grandfather was trying to protect."

She glanced over at him and saw the taut planes of his face relax and soften as he leaned forward to watch the pair, his arms crossed on top of the steering wheel.

"I read a book entitled *Green Mansions* when I was a child," she breathed. "Although it was set in Venezuela, it told the story of an unspoiled wilderness a lot like this."

"And of a wild bird girl named Rima, who lived there in harmony with nature."

"You've read it?" Her eyes widened.

"I'm not illiterate." He leaned back in the seat to turn the key in the ignition, the hardness returning to his face.

The doe and her fawn, startled by the sound, snapped alert and bounded into the greenery.

"I never said—" she tried to protest, but he cut her short as he shifted into drive.

"Look, I'm not any happier about this arrangement than you are." He pressed the accelerator hard and swung the Jeep around a mud-slick curve with a ferocity that made Allison clutch her seat. "Once the will is read, I will gladly see you onto the next flight to Toronto. But for now, let's declare a truce. I don't have the time or energy to keep sparring with you." He slowed the Jeep and shot her a sideways glance, one eyebrow raised.

He was right. Keeping up a verbal battle neither of them appeared destined to win was pointless. Allison eased her fingernails out of the cracked upholstery, met his look, and nodded. "Truce."

When the Jeep jolted into the Lodge grounds, her breath caught in her throat. Again, she'd forgotten how wonderful it was.

Surrounded by manicured lawns luminously green in the fog, the rambling single-story log structure with its full-length front veranda faced the North Passage River. Behind it were two other log structures—the caretaker's small cottage, where she suspected Heath now lived, and a large barnlike building that served as a storage shed and housed the generator that provided power for the Lodge.

The estate's only other structure, the boathouse where her grandfather had died, was farther down river, hidden in the trees. The remembrance of the place sent a shiver coursing up her spine. *Get over it. Just get over it.* To quell her memories, she returned her attention to the Lodge.

A wide fieldstone chimney rose from the ground to beyond the peak of the roof on the end facing the driveway. A wave of nostalgia engulfed her. The last night she'd spent with her grandfather in the Lodge had been before a blazing fire on the hearth that chimney vented. They had listened to rain bucketing down on the roof, and he'd told her stories about the birds and plants and animals that were at home in his bit of wilderness. He'd explained he named the area the Chance because it offered people a chance to enjoy all that was good and beautiful in the wilderness, and, as her mother had said, the chance to find themselves, their purpose in life.

She'd only half listened, her thoughts on the events of the previous evening, down at the boathouse, and the creature who'd torn up all her romantic dreams and trampled them into the mud.

God, how I loathe Heath Oakes.

Allison brought her reminiscences up short. Reminiscences she couldn't afford to harbor, not if she wanted to make a clean break from the place.

Heath braked the Jeep at the rear entrance and got out. While he was retrieving her suitcase, Allison scrambled to release her seatbelt, swing her legs out over the side, and slip to the ground, her skirt riding up her thighs. By the time he joined her, she'd managed to pull it back into place and stood waiting for him as intact as she could be, her once-fashionable suit soaking up mist like a sponge.

"Come on." He hefted her luggage and headed up the steps. "Let's get inside."

Allison took a moment to look around the grounds and spotted a gleaming new Cherokee parked at the rear of the house.

"Visitors?" she asked.

"Belongs to the Lodge." He paused to look back at her.

"Then you didn't have to bring that thing," she jerked a finger back at the old Jeep behind them.

"No. Just wanted to. Thought Jack would appreciate the gesture. Come on, let's get inside."

****

25

They stood in the kitchen she remembered so well. Nothing much had changed. The long room, with its lengths of spotless counters and cupboards, its built-in range tops and wall ovens, rows of gleaming pots and pans hanging above them, still had double refrigerator-freezers and a pair of dishwashers. Best of all, everything sparkled from cleaning and maintenance. Mrs. Oakes must be all her grandfather had bragged her up to be.

The kitchen, like the rest of the lodge, was paneled in knotty pine that complemented the long, wide planks of its birch flooring. A row of windows above the stoves and double sink offered an excellent view of the manicured lawns and carefully pruned forest at the back of the Lodge. Jack Adams had spared no expense to make the room convenient and pleasant. He'd always declared a contented cook was a good cook and his guests deserved no less.

While she'd been taking in her surroundings, Heath had put down her suitcase and removed his work boots. Now he straightened up.

"Come on," he said. "I'll show you to your room. You should get out of those wet clothes and into a hot shower."

The suggestion sounded like an offer of heaven. She stepped out of the boots that had shredded the feet and ankles of her pantyhose and followed him through the long dining room, trying not to hobble.

Blisters. Blisters so big I have blisters on them.

The room had remained furnished with a long, antique mahogany dining table, matching chairs, and a beautiful handcarved sideboard that served as a buffet table. A series of gleaming hot trays, now cold and empty, graced its top. China cabinets along the back wall stood filled with dishes adorned with wildlife motifs Jack and Maud had had especially made for the Lodge. Several garden doors forming most of the front wall offered an unobstructed view of the river. Everything reflected the same measure of care as the kitchen.

Heath led her down the familiar corridor at the back of the dining room. Six guest rooms with full baths opened from each side. At the end, behind a closed door, was her grandparents' private suite.

Allison paused and stared at it until she realized Heath had opened the door of the first guest room and was waiting for her to precede him inside.

"I was thinking…"

"About Jack," he said, putting her suitcase down at the foot of the bed.

"And Gram," she replied gazing around the room. Little had changed. Like all the guest rooms she remembered, it exuded warmth and cozy comfort. The old-fashioned bedroom suite, with its wide dresser and mirror, quilt-covered sleigh bed, and maple rocking chair, made it homey and welcoming. She ran her hand over the rolled wood of the bed's footboard, a faint smile on her lips. "Gram loved this house, every inch of it."

"What about you?" Heath watched her from the doorway.

"I never stayed long enough to form an attachment." She snapped back the lie. "Now, if you'll excuse me, I'd like to get out of these wet clothes."

"You'll find a guest robe in the bath, miss." He swept her a mocking bow and backed out, closing the

27

door with catlike quiet behind him.

Damn him. Trying to make me uncomfortable. Allison strode into the bathroom, unbuttoning her suit jacket with a violence that all but ripped the hand-covered buttons from its front. *Sarcastic bastard! That truce is straining at the bit already.*

Fifteen minutes later, she padded barefoot into the bedroom. Swathed in one of the Lodge's white terry robes, her freshly shampooed hair blown dry, she felt much better, much more ready to cope with the barbarian whom her grandfather had made his foreman.

"Slippers, I need slippers." She rummaged though the suitcase he'd thrown onto the bed. Only when she'd found a pair and was bending to put them on did she notice that the black suit she'd worn earlier, that she'd left draped over a chair, was gone.

Mrs. Oakes. That's it. She came into my room and took my suit out to dry. I hope she's not a meddler who sticks her nose into my business. I don't need that kind of nuisance. Her son is bad enough. Wonder where she was when we arrived, why she didn't come out to meet us? And why wasn't she at the funeral? After all Gramps did for her and her despicable child, it was the least she could have done. Until that moment she'd been too involved with other thoughts to wonder about the housekeeper.

As she passed through the dining room and glanced outside toward the river, she noticed fog still lay wrapped over the landscape. Although the Lodge was warm and she could hear the crackle of a wood fire from the living room hearth, she shivered. Thank goodness Mrs. Oakes was on the premises. Being alone under such eerie conditions with the last man to see her

28

grandfather alive would not be a heartening prospect. She pushed her way through the swinging door into the kitchen. Heath stood at the stove. He was stirring the contents of a pot.

"Where's your mother?"

"Took you long enough to ask." He kept his attention on his task.

"It's been an unusual day. I had other things on my mind. I assumed she was here at the Lodge taking care of things while you helped bury Gramps. So where is she?"

"England." Concentrating on what he was cooking, he didn't turn to face her.

"England! Good lord, what is she doing in England?" *Drop a bombshell or what!*

"My grandmother was a war bride. My mother always wanted to trace her roots over there. The trip was a gift from Jack…just before he died."

"You mean we're alone here? No guests, no housekeeper?" *Can this day get any more insane?*

"That's right." He lifted a steaming spoonful from the pot and held it up to cool.

"This is incredible." Allison threw up her arms dismay. "My mother will be furious when she finds out."

"She knows." He tasted from the spoon, dropped it into the sink, and faced her.

"What? No way! Why would she allow me to come here, knowing…?"

"I think she considers us both mature, responsible adults." He shrugged and leaned back against the counter, crossing his arms on his chest. "And you do have that self-defense course."

"Don't tempt me." She clutched the shawl collar of her robe to her throat. "I'm going to call her right now and let her know the situation, because I think you're lying."

"You'll have to go to town to do that." His lips quirked. "We didn't have a telephone when you were here years ago, and we still don't. Jack always figured having one would only be an unnecessary intrusion. And cells don't work up here because of our location between the mountains."

"You mean the only way to contact civilization is still that old CB he kept…keeps…in his office?"

"Once in a while, when it decides to work. By the way, you don't have to clutch that robe. I'm not about to ravish you. At least not until I've had my supper."

"Ohhh!" She dropped her hand to her side to glare at him. "Very funny."

"Your knuckles were turning white. Couldn't have been very comfortable."

He turned back to his cooking.

Don't let him get to you. Don't!

She cocked her head to one side. "Is that a dryer I hear? You're doing laundry?"

"Not mine," he replied, bending to check something that was wafting a mouth-watering fragrance from the oven. "I threw your suit in to dry."

"No!" Allison bolted past him and into the laundry room. Yanking open the dryer door, she stared in horror at the tangled black ball. She pulled it out and strode into the kitchen.

"Look, just look!" She shoved it in front of him. "This suit was especially designed and tailored for me. Now, not even a midget could get it on."

"Not something you'd wear around here anyhow." He shrugged and returned his attention to the stove. "So no big loss."

"Ahhhhh!" Allison bundled the shrunken suit under her arm and headed back to her bedroom. *Barbarian, barbarian, barbarian.*

****

"Dinner." He stood in the open doorway of her bedroom, a large slotted spoon in one hand, an oven mitt on the other.

Wonder what he'd look like in an apron? Only an apron. Damn! Where did that come from? Focus, Allison. Focus on the royal pain he really is.

"I need to find something to wear." In an effort to change her thought pattern, she began to dig in the suitcase on her bed.

"Don't take too long." He turned back toward the kitchen.

By the time she entered the dining room, wearing designer jeans and a green silk shirt, he'd placed two steaming plates on the table. Candles in its center cast bewitching shadows in the gathering gloom of the foggy spring twilight.

Is he trying to romance me? Well, good luck with that. He may be the best-looking wild-woods type I've ever seen, but I know what's behind the fancy cover. Heath Oakes is one book I don't want as bedtime reading.

"Smells like you may be able to cook." She drew a deep inhale.

"You be the judge." He took a decanter from the sideboard and poured white wine into each of their long-stemmed glasses. "The asparagus and rice are my doing. The Chicken Kiev is from the freezer. Before my mother left, she prepared it along with some other dishes to keep me from starvation."

They ate in silence. Allison was content with the situation. Words between them had a way of degenerating into nasty remarks and personal insults.

****

"That was excellent." Allison finished the meal and touched the napkin to her lips.

"Glad you enjoyed it." He stood and gathered the plates and utensils. "Coffee in the living room. I've got a fire going in there."

Touching remembered furniture and pictures along the way, Allison wandered to the adjoining room. At the archway that separated dining and living areas, she slid open the bifold doors that divided the two. And caught her breath.

The big room lined with varnished pine and floored with gleaming birch glowed golden in the soft light of the flames dancing in the wide fieldstone hearth that dominated the room. A long, chocolate-colored couch and an oak coffee table filled the area in front of the fireplace. On the opposite wall, a well-filled bookcase stretched from floor to ceiling. To its left, a closed door led to what Allison remembered was her grandfather's office. Scattered around the spacious room in friendly conversational groupings were matching easy chairs, each with an end table holding its own oil lamp as the center piece. A pair of hurricane lamps decorated the mantel.

Allison remembered her grandfather had not permitted the installation of electric lights in this room. He'd wanted his guests to experience the romance of a pioneer ambience in a homely atmosphere.

Homely. Like home. The thought rose up to describe her overall impression. But that was ridiculous. Home for Allison Armstrong was an ultramodern glass-and-chrome condo situated on the seventeenth floor of a security building in the heart of Toronto. Home was an hour's drive from her parents' spacious multilevel in the suburbs and another half hour's drive from the stable where she boarded her horse. Allison's Pride was an elegant Kentucky-bred chestnut hunter with a family tree that would impress the most discriminating of equine enthusiasts.

It wasn't this log hostelry in the backwoods.

Pulling herself out of her thoughts, she crossed the room and curled up on the couch to stare into the flames crackling on the hearth.

"Coffee." Heath walked into the room with a wooden tray holding a pot and mugs with pheasant motifs. He placed it on the table in front of the fire and poured dark, steaming liquid into the cups.

"Cream, sugar?"

"Black."

"I should have guessed."

"And just what is that supposed to mean?" She tried to remain cool as she lifted her cup from the tray.

"Everything with you has to be black and white. Good or bad. Worthwhile or garbage. No gray areas for Ms. Armstrong, CFO."

It's on. Oh, it's definitely on, Mister He-Man Woodsman.

"You think you know me so well, don't you." She plunked her cup down onto the coffee table and jumped to her feet. "You have no idea who I am, who I've become. But as soon as Gramps' will is read, you'll learn a whole lot more."

"Good. I like a surprise."

"When is the will to be read?" She swallowed her reflexive response and managed a semblance of civility. "Super soon, I hope."

"Tomorrow around noon." He sat down in front of the fire, weathered fingers clasping his cup. "You'll be able to catch the four o'clock flight."

"Good. Great, in fact. As soon as I get back to T-O I'll contact National Realty and set up the sale of this place. You'd better start packing. I'll want you out asap."

She turned to sweep out of the room, remembered her coffee, and hesitated. It was good, one of the best brews she'd ever tasted. And she hadn't had a cup since breakfast. She swung back, scooped up the mug, then made a second attempt at a haughty exit.

"Don't let thoughts of what Jack might have left to me disturb your sleep. The only thing he promised me was his favorite old salmon rod." His words, tinged with sarcastic humor followed her.

Chapter Three

"Gramps left you a fishing rod?"

"Yes." He freshened his coffee. "Years ago, when I caught my first salmon on that rod and Jack showed me the right way to release it back into the river, he said he'd leave it to me in his will. He always kept his promises."

"How do I know you're telling the truth?"

"You don't." He shrugged. "And neither do I…until tomorrow."

Keep your cool. In less than twenty-four hours, you'll be rid of him forever.

In an effort to take her own advice, Allison ambled over to the bookcase and began to peruse the contents.

"*The Lost Will.*" She pulled a volume from the shelves and waved it in his direction. "As I recall, a man is murdered by a prospective heir. Think I'll climb into bed and refresh my memory."

As she sauntered out of the living room, thumbing through its pages in pretense of a casual confidence she was far from feeling, he called after her, "That's a Christie, isn't it? See if it mentions anything about a twenty-year-old salmon rod as a motive. Dame Agatha generally used bigger gains as motives, as *I* recall."

Allison's lips tightened as she crossed the darkened dining room. Her fingers gripped the novel with a vengeance.

I wish you were a hero-woodsman type swinging through the woods. I'd be first in line to trip you up.

Inside her warm room, she snapped on the light. Heath must have activated the electric heat. Even though it was the first of May, a damp, foggy night in this area could be chilly, even frosty.

She pulled a skimpy silk nightgown from her suitcase. Not exactly appropriate to the setting. A wicked desire to see the expression on her companion's face if she paraded out into the living room wearing it slipped across her mind.

Not tonight, but maybe just before I kick him off my property. She laid it aside.

Another bit of pink, this time in a floral pattern, caught her eye. Rose-patterned flannel pajamas.

When Myra had suggested warm sleepwear might come in handy on their trip to New Brunswick, Allison had laughed. They'd be staying at a motel in town for two nights, for heaven's sake. She, Allison Armstrong, was accustomed to the sensation of silk against her skin in bed. But she hadn't been expecting to be left in the backwoods with a barbarian named Heath Oakes.

You really set me up to stay here, didn't you, Mom. I wonder when you stuck this kiddie outfit into my suitcase. No doubt about keeping things platonic in this getup. Not even Nature Boy-slash-gigolo could be turned on by it.

What the heck. She gave the jacket a flap and picked up the pants. No one was going to see her in them, and it was only for one night. Late tomorrow afternoon she'd be on a plane headed back to the city.

Dragging the flannel outfit behind her, she went to the window and drew the drapes against the fog and darkness. Five minutes later, she climbed into the sleigh bed, pulled the quilts about her, adjusted the shade on the bedside lamp, and settled down to read *The Lost Will*, her pajamas and white cotton gym socks cozy and comforting in the inhospitable night.

The digits on the clock radio beside her bed indicated 9:15 p.m. Normally Allison Armstrong wouldn't be in bed for at least another two hours. This particular day had been exhausting, though, with the early morning flight out of Ottawa, the difficulty in renting a car at the small-town airport, the emotional impact of the funeral, that surreal pilgrimage to the gravesite in the fog, and, finally, this enforced cohabitation with the person she detested most on the face of the earth. It made the warm cocoon of room and bed welcome at an early hour. She was turning page twelve in her novel when the book slipped from her hands and she slept.

She awoke with a start. Surprised that she'd been asleep, she glanced at the bedside clock radio. Midnight. With a sigh she picked up the book. She was trying to find her place when a sound from somewhere in the Lodge caught her attention. Someone or something was moving around inside the building.

A bear! A ravenous, fresh-out-of-hibernation bear! But a bear would have had to break glass to get in. She'd have heard it. Whatever it was, it was being stealthy, moving quietly out of the kitchen (she guessed from the direction of the sound), across the dining room, into the living room, and probably—her mind clicked into gear—toward the office. A robber looking for money in the obvious place! A miserable lowlife out to steal from her Gramps.

Allison recalled her grandparents had always provided a flashlight in each guest room. Incensed, she pulled one from the drawer of her nightstand and snapped off the bedside lamp.

She hesitated a few seconds, until her eyes became accustomed to the dark; then, heart pounding, she slid out of bed and tiptoed to the door. Without turning on the flashlight, she eased out into the corridor. The rain and fog must have cleared. Ahead she could see moonlight streaming across the dining room.

As she tiptoed forward on stockinged feet, she saw a thin shaft of light stretching out into the living room from the all-but-closed office doorway. She'd been right! It was a burglar, a bit of scum who couldn't wait until Jack Adams was cold in his grave to make his move.

Outrage overcame apprehension. She'd teach this miserable trash to violate her Gramps' possessions!

Holding the foot-long flashlight above her head as a club, Allison moved cat-quiet across the shadowy room. At the office door she paused, every drop of adrenaline in her body ready to charge.

She couldn't see the person inside. He or she was hidden by the nearly closed door. The last ounce of sane logic she possessed tried to tell her it would be best to get a look at her opposition before she attacked. It failed. Yelling like a banshee, she kicked open the door and leaped on the figure bending over a computer connection.

"Hey!" As the pair tumbled to the floor, Allison recognized his voice.

His arm, thrown up and back in a reflexive gesture of defense, knocked the flashlight from her hand.

"Sneaking, underhanded bastard!" She tried to land a blow against the side of his head with a clenched fist.

Feline swift, he caught her wrist and pulled her arm to her side. Her left hand he'd already immobilized behind her back. He was too fast for any of the self-defense moves she'd learned.

"Let me up, you sniveling piece of trash!" She was sputtering as she lay trapped beneath his body. "How dare you go through Gramps' office! It's private! It belongs to his family! You have no right here, you money-grubbing gigolo!"

She glared up into his golden brown eyes as they narrowed into predatory slits. Her breath clogged in her throat. *I've gone too far. Oh, God, this time I've gone too far.*

"Money-grubbing gigolo? Is that what you think I am?" He was breathing hard. "Okay, I'll give you a sample of what I have to offer and let you decide if the ladies are getting good value for their dollar!"

His mouth came down over hers in a sudden, all-out kiss, his body covering hers with its hard, virile length.

"No!" She tried to protest, but he held her fast, probing tongue muffling her words, body moving over hers in a slow, primitive motion that made her react as she wouldn't have believed possible seconds earlier.

In a flash she spun away into a realm of sensual intensity she'd never known existed. Logic, common sense, and animosity all dissolved like ice in a microwave.

The man personified earthy virility, feral and elemental as the wilderness that surrounded them. Her needs, basic and erotic, overwhelmed her, and she was lost to his kisses, his undulating body that promised more, so much more. When he freed her arms, they went up and about his neck.

In a single, lithe movement he twisted free of her embrace and to his feet to stand looking down at her, arms crossed on his chest in a lord-of-the-wilderness stance. His face registered disgust. "Good value, or what?"

"Street trash!" She scrambled to her feet. "You haven't changed at all! How could you…"

"How could I what?" His eyes became amber slits. "Defend myself? Offer you proof of the validity of your accusations? Don't try to lie about it. You liked it, Ms. CFO. You liked it a lot. I know the signs."

"I did not!"

He shrugged, turned away, and knelt again to resume his work on the computer connection.

"I want you to leave…" Her entire body still reflexing from his assault, she sputtered.

"Not until I find out if the Lodge has a mortgage hanging over it," he muttered, plugging in a connection. He drew a deep, exasperated breath as he looked at the diagonal lines crossing the monitor. "James Wilcox told me the Chance is heavily mortgaged and if the person who inherits doesn't manage to meet an upcoming balloon payment, it'll go on the auction block in less than a month."

"The real estate agent said that?" Allison's anger vanished into shock. "I can't believe Gramps would ever mortgage anything. He remembered the Great Depression too well and never took out loans on anything."

"I don't believe it either." He tried another

connection, with no better results. "Still, forewarned is forearmed. We need the facts, and they're all right in this miserable pile of nuts and screws."

"Here, let me." Coming back into self-control, she had to know the truth as well. She knelt beside him, took the wires from his hands, and snapped them into the proper slots. The lines on the monitor straightened.

"There." She slid into the chair in front of the screen. "Let's check out accounts payable."

"You sound as if you actually know something about this." He got up, pulled another office chair close beside her, and sat down.

"I'm CFO of a large corporation. I majored in business administration at university. I take it you studied something else."

"Biology, ecology, nothing important."

"Okay, okay. Point." Biting back a more caustic retort, she punched a few keys and waited. *Stop distracting me!* His tanned, clean-shaven jaw and softly curling hair were too close to her right cheek for comfort. "Move back and let me work."

"Fine." Raising his hands, he backed off and went to lean against a file cabinet, arms and ankles crossed.

Fifteen minutes later Allison settled back in the chair and swiveled it to face him. "No mortgages, not even an unpaid gas bill. Wilcox was attempting a snow job. And a pretty clumsy one. He should have known I'd look into the accounts as soon as I got here."

"Just as I thought." He rolled his shoulders and Allison realized he'd had a long day, too. "Jack left his finances in the same great shape he left everything on this place. I'm glad I won't have to start issuing checks for the Chance's expenses until the end of the month.

I'll need to get a handle on this computer stuff before I do."

"You? Issue checks? What were you, his business manager? If so, you should have been a lot better informed about the state of his finances."

"I was his guide foreman, his camp manager." He shrugged. "Finances aren't a strong point with me, but he did give me his power of attorney several years ago in case checks had to be issued when he wasn't around. I didn't want the responsibility, but he insisted."

"I see." Allison turned off the computer and stood. "So now you sneak around in the middle of the night, trying to access his financial records to see how large a check his bank account can handle."

"Do you really believe that?" A sardonic grin curled his lips.

"Does it matter? After tomorrow you'll be out of my life forever. Lock the door when you leave."

She was crossing the living room when his shadow fell over her. Glancing back, she saw him lounging in the lighted office doorway, watching her.

"What?" The word snapped out.

"I never thought I could be turned on by pink flannel," he said, his face suffused in shadow. "Until now."

"Ahhhhhhh!" The man was a lecher. She wished she were wearing work boots so she could stomp away.

Back in her room, she locked the door and climbed into bed. *Tramp, savage...* The words were among her last conscious thoughts as she pulled the quilts up to her chin and settled once more for the night. The positive aspect of the entire situation was that tomorrow she'd be rid of him.

Still, the memory of that kiss on the office floor, the sensation of his body covering hers… It sent her dreaming the moment sleep overtook her, dreaming of a tall, lean, muscular man of the jungle. Clad only in a loincloth, arms crossed on his hard, bare chest, he confronted her in the green tunnel of foliage leading to the Chance, blocking her way, making her innards come alive with what felt like the wings of a hundred frantic butterflies. Desperately she ordered him out of her path. Then she caught the gleam in his eyes.

Her heart rate raced off, the bit of reason clamped in the teeth of desire. Melting like butter on a hot muffin, she realized she was wearing rain-soaked pink flannel pajamas and oversized rubber boots. And while he seemed to be standing in dazzling sunlight, she was under a cloudburst.

Then he was moving toward her, as lithe and soundless as a panther, his gaze hot with primitive fire. Allison caught her breath and waited, understanding for the first time what true animal magnetism was.

Heart pounding, she watched as he came to her… Then, passing her, brushed her aside to embrace Candace Breckenridge, who'd apparently been standing behind her. As he was reaching to draw the eager woman into his arms, Allison jerked awake.

Cursed dream! Strike that! Damned nightmare. She raised herself up on one elbow and pummeled her pillow.

"Blast him!" she muttered. "Blast him, the miserable womanizing tramp! Tomorrow, as soon as that lawyer reads the will and Heath Oakes is in full, legal possession of his fishing rod, I'll send him packing so fast he'll be dizzy!"

Chapter Four

Allison woke to a spring breeze and a robin's song wafting in her open window. Sunlight peeked under the undulating curtains to make moving patches of gleaming amber on the polished hardwood floor.

Where am I? Oh, right. At the Lodge. She yawned and stretched. It felt good to be there.

Then a thought struck her and she sat bolt upright. She hadn't gone to sleep with the window open. *He* must have used his manager's pass key to come into her room while she was asleep. *What a nerve!* She bounded out of bed and headed for the bathroom.

In front of the dresser mirror she paused and fluffed her hair. *How did I look when he was in here?* She threw up her hands. *What is wrong with you, Allison Armstrong? As if it mattered. As if you cared.* With a disgusted growl, she strode into the bathroom, locked the door, and shed those pajamas he'd deemed sexy.

Fifteen minutes later, dressed in jeans, sweatshirt, and sneakers, she entered the kitchen. The aroma of more of the delicious coffee she remembered from the previous evening greeted her, along with a note from Heath that informed her milk, juice, cream, croissants, and homemade strawberry jam were in the refrigerator, bacon and eggs, too, if she felt like cooking.

She didn't. She poured coffee and juice, buttered a

croissant, and carried it all into the dining room.

First she tried sitting in her grandfather's place, but it didn't feel right. Next she tried Heath's chair on the right.

Definitely, no.

Then, feeling like Goldilocks in the forest home of the three bears, she moved to her grandmother's place at the foot of the massive table. *Ah, yes*. With a sigh she settled to her breakfast.

When she'd finished, she put her cup, glass, and saucer in the dishwasher and headed out the back door to find Heath. They had to talk before the lawyer got here.

She paused with her hand on the knob as she saw her grandfather's favorite sheepskin-lined rancher's jacket hanging on a peg behind the door. Impulsively she snatched it up, pulled it on, and turned back to the breadbox on the counter near the window for a slice of bread. Every morning Gramps had taken a piece of bread out to the bold jays he called Whiskey Jacks.

When the birds saw her, they descended, silent as snowflakes. She didn't flatter herself on the attraction. The bread had garnered their interest. When they landed about her feet, she knelt to offer each a chunk and wondered if Heath fed them, too. Had he cared enough to carry on Jack's concern for local wildlife?

Enough! Come noon, her mother would be sole owner of the Chance, and the Armstrongs could legally send one mighty Oakes packing.

She let the last bird snatch the remaining bit of crust from her fingers before she arose and headed for the small log cottage Heath and his mother shared.

The inner door was open. When Allison went up

the three short steps she could see a small, neat kitchen through the screen and hear music playing softly from a radio on the counter near the sink.

"Heath?" she called through the mesh door. "Are you in there?"

The only answer was the announcer's voice at the end of the song, telling his listeners not to be deceived by the fine morning. More rain and fog were on the way.

Presented with an opportunity, Allison's curiosity flared. Easing open the screen she slipped inside.

The kitchen held an apartment-sized refrigerator, stove, and a cozy breakfast nook built into one wall below a window that looked out into the forest. Hand-quilted placemats with a wildflower design decorated its Formica tabletop and matched the seat and back cushions of a rocking chair near the opposite window, the ruffled curtains, and a tea cozy covering a pot on the counter. Framed needlepoint floral designs decorated the walls above the cupboards.

How could the woman who had made this welcoming place also be responsible for the creation of Heath the Barbarian? Allison shook her head and tiptoed down the short hall at the back of the room.

The open door at its end revealed a small, tidy bathroom. Two others, one to her left, the other to her right, she guessed led to bedrooms. Opening the door to her right, she saw a bed covered with a dusty rose spread that matched the window drapes and a mahogany dresser with neatly laid-out toiletries, a large wicker basket of needlepoint materials nestled against its side. She closed the door and turned to open the one opposite.

That room contained a large bed covered with a patchwork quilt, plain white window curtains, a wide dresser with only a hairbrush on its polished surface, a well-filled floor-to-ceiling bookcase against the rear wall, and a chair and desk in one corner.

Papers neatly stacked on the latter intrigued her. She tiptoed over to get a better look.

To her disappointment, they appeared to be purely business, letters from people seeking reservations or information about the Lodge, repair estimates, competitive prices on canoes, paddles, groceries, and the like.

Something pink in the wastebasket beside the desk caught her attention. A letter. She couldn't resist. She bent and picked it up. The delicate blue handwriting and light scent of expensive perfume assured her it was no business document. Her heart racing, she began to read.

It was a love letter filled with reminiscences of intimate moments spent with none other than Heath Oakes. Allison felt a hot gush of anger crawling up her neck and face. It was signed, "All my love, C.B." Candace Breckenridge?

Nausea roiled in her stomach. Accusing Heath of this kind of liaison was one thing; finding absolute proof was another.

"What do you think you're doing?"

She whirled to face Heath framed in the doorway. The piece of pink paper slid from her fingers and fluttered to the floor.

"Nothing…I…that is…"

"I wouldn't call reading someone else's personal mail nothing."

He crossed the room and snatched up the letter to wave it under her nose. "This is none of your business, Ms. Armstrong. None at all."

"Your turning the Chance into a spa where lonely middle-aged *married* women can live out their romantic fantasies is," she exploded back at him, although inwardly she was unnerved by his blazing eyes and clenched fists. "This is a respectable lodge, not some…some…"

"So you think this just confirms what you suspected, that I'm a backwoods gigolo who fools around with the wives and partners of the men who come up here?"

"Are you telling me none of what is in that letter ever happened, that this woman is lying? Oh, come off it!"

"Show me where it says we had an actual affair, that we slept together. Go on, show me."

Allison re-read. He was right. Nowhere did Candace refer to an actual affair. But that wasn't proof.

"I happen to know this woman." She glared up into his mocking expression. "She's much too smart to commit anything to paper that could be used as evidence in a divorce court. You see, Nature Boy, while she might enjoy a two-week fling with you and your muscles, Candace Breckenridge is not about to risk her comfortable lifestyle for you."

"She never did." He pulled the letter from her hand and threw it back into the wastepaper can. "Nothing she or I did constituted infidelity. She's just a lonely, neglected woman who wants to feel attractive and desirable, who wants to be listened to with interest and genuinely cared about."

"And you managed all that…on a purely platonic level? Quick, let me look outside. There must be a few white crows around."

"So now I'm a liar, too." He turned and sauntered over to his bookcase with amazing, icy calm. "Would you like to borrow a book while you're here? I'm a fan of murder mysteries. I'm sure that somewhere in my collection you'll find a scenario that matches Jack's death to a T. Then you'll be able to promote me from gigolo and liar to killer."

He swung back to face her, his move swift and catlike. His eyes had narrowed, his lean bronzed face gone hard and cold.

"I never said…suggested…" Her heart bumping against her ribs, she began to back toward the door.

"No, but you thought…and thought…and thought." He slammed it shut, then held her trapped against it, his hands on the panel on either side of her head, towering over her, making her shrink before his pure animal power. "Let me add a bit more color to the picture you've painted of me." His tone became dangerously soft. "I have a criminal record. I've spent time in prison. Do outlaws turn you on, Allison Armstrong? Do they?"

He was all but touching her now, so close she felt she was drowning in smoldering amber pools and a rock hard wall of muscle and sinew. His nearness frightened her, excited her, left her gasping.

"Don't…" The word was a strangled whisper. Her heart raced out of control, partly in fear, but mostly— she hated herself for it—in wild anticipation. She remembered his kiss, that earthy, head-spinning, belly- turning kiss on the floor the previous night, and her knees turned to mush.

"What do you really believe about me, Allie?" He astonished her with his use of the pet name her grandfather had given her years ago. "In your heart?"

"I think..." she breathed softly, looking up at him with what she hoped was a beseeching look. "That I couldn't hate you more." She lunged out with both hands and a knee.

"Ahhhh!" He stumbled backwards, and she yanked open the door.

"I believe you're a conceited, money-mongering ape!" she yelled as she ran, stumbling, out of the cottage.

Chapter Five

She paused a few yards from the cottage and glanced back to see if he was pursuing her. He wasn't. She threw back her shoulders, sucked in a deep breath, and gave herself a figurative pat on the back.

I showed him. He won't mess with me again. Wobbly knees and pounding heart be darned. I showed him who's in charge around here.

A smug little smile on her lips, she headed for the boat house. As she made her way over the root-roughened foot path carpeted with pine needles, childhood memories flooded back, and she slowed her pace. She and Gramps had walked this trail so many times when she was a little girl. Sometimes she'd put her small hand in his large one and enjoy the sense of warmth and security. Other times she'd skip ahead of him, making him laugh at her antics.

When she reached the boathouse, she pulled his jacket about her and sat down on the weathered old park bench near its open doorway. In spite of the sunlight bathing her in a soft pool of warmth, she recognized the cold nip in the air that characterized the early reluctance of spring in this country. With a sigh she turned up the woolly collar, stuffed cold fingers beneath her armpits, and cuddled into a corner. She needed time to think, time to straighten out the tangle of thoughts and emotions Heath Oakes had snarled about

51

her mind.

She gazed out at the river rushing past, glinting in the sun. Jack Adams had loved the North Passage and gloried in all its moods and caprices.

"It was meant to continue forever," he'd said, his arm about his granddaughter as they'd sat together on this same bench over a dozen years ago. "Like life through a family."

And she was all that was left to keep their family going. She and...Paul? Somehow she couldn't bring him into focus as a viable current in the stream that was the Adams dynasty.

A squirrel scampered down a tree trunk and sat up on its haunches in front of her. It stared at her with wide, inquisitive eyes. Memory rushed back...Sammy, the baby squirrel she'd spent hours nursing through babyhood during her last summer at the Chance.

She'd been fourteen the summer she'd found Sammy lying helpless at the bottom of a tree. When she could find no nest to return him to, she'd carried him back to the Lodge. With her grandfather's help, she'd made a tiny bed for him, a piece of blanket in an empty screwdriver box.

At Jack's instruction, she'd dug out a doll's bottle from among her discarded toys and begun feeding the little creature. Three weeks later she and Jack had released a nearly adult Sammy back into the forest, fit and ready for his life on the Chance.

The memory brought another into her mind. The memory of how she'd glanced up one day, as she sat feeding Sammy on the veranda steps, to see sixteen-year-old Heath slouched into a James Dean stance against a tree, hips thrust forward, thumbs hooked into the pockets of faded jeans as he watched her.

Something in those intense eyes had sent her adolescent body into a whirl, awakening a myriad of sensations. He'd been the embodiment of every teenage girl's romantic bad-boy image.

I was one stupid kid. Dragging up memories isn't any good. Heath Oakes was an inner-city hoodlum. All that changed is that now he's a wilderness hoodlum. As soon as Gramps' will is read and the Armstrongs are legally in possession of the Chance, I'll kick him out of my life once and for all.

She got up from the bench and headed back to the Lodge, her strides long and determined.

At noon, dressed in the black suit she'd worn to the funeral, Allison placed a plate of sandwiches on the dining room table. She winced as she passed a mirror. Skirt and jacket looked as if she'd poured herself into them, thanks to that barbarian and his dryer. She'd had no choice. It was the only outfit she had that was suitable for a somber occasion like a will reading. The jeans and tops she'd brought and worn on the plane were far too casual, intended only for comfort after months of business suits and high heels.

She glanced down at the jacket straining at its buttons. *Thanks to that stupid savage, I look like some kind of kinky hooker.*

She headed back into the kitchen to check on the coffee. Giving the too-short skirt a downward tug, she pushed through the swinging door.

"Good morning." Heath stood leaning against the counter, arms crossed on his chest. Dressed in a charcoal suit, white shirt, gray silk tie, and shining black dress shoes, only the below-the-ears hair and weather-bronzed complexion gave evidence of his woodsman persona. His gaze meandered over her from head to foot, one corner of his mouth quirking upward.

"Oh, right!" She stopped short and planted her feet apart, hands on her hips. "Make me look bad, why don't you. Where was that get-up yesterday? It's what you should have worn to the funeral."

"To drive a tractor down a mud bog of a road and shovel in a grave?" He raised an eyebrow.

"Well…" She strode over to the coffeemaker and checked its progress. When she glanced at him, she saw him watching her with that catlike intensity she was coming to know only too well. *It's as if he can see right down into my deepest thoughts and emotions.*

"What are you planning to do once the will is read?" He snapped her out of her inane thoughts.

"Catch the next flight home." She reached for cups on the top shelf and felt her skirt ride up. Grabbing at it, she stepped back.

"Here, let me." He brushed past her with a scent of something like the forest after a spring shower. Or a really nice masculine soap.

"How many?" He'd paused with a pair of cups in his hands, looking down at her with those mesmerizing golden-brown eyes.

"What? Oh, four should be enough. I'm not sure if the lawyer will be coming alone. Best to be prepared." Her words stumbled. *I'm CFO of a major corporation. I'm the first female executive they've had in one hundred and fifty years of operation. Now this…this savage is turning me into a stuttering teenager just by smelling half-decent and looking…*

"Saucers?" He placed four cups on the counter.

"What? Oh, right, of course, saucers."

"There you go." He put them beside the cups but didn't move away from her. "Now back to our previous conversation. You know I was asking what you'll do with the Chance." His words were hard and clipped this time, even as his continued proximity made butterflies burst from cocoons in the centre of her body.

"Still a little cranky from our scuffle this morning, are we?" She pulled herself out of his sphere of control and sauntered across the kitchen to take coffee spoons from a drawer. *Getting back in the game, girl. Good for you.*

"Old news. Right now I'm concerned about seeing Jack's wishes carried out."

"I assume my mother, being his only child, will inherit everything…except the legendary salmon rod." She swung to face him. "When she does, she'll have no choice but to sell. She's not about to leave my father in order to operate this place, and he can't relocate here."

"Jack wanted the Chance to stay in his family."

"That's not going to happen."

"You could take it over." He moved to tower above her. "You're supposed to be a financial wizard, a pioneer female executive in that company of yours, according to Jack."

"Me? Take on this place?" The words were a gusty exhale. "Are you crazy?"

"You've got a responsibility to Jack's memory." He strode over to the percolator and took a mug from a cupboard above it. "What did you leave behind in Toronto? A high-priced chrome-and-glass apartment and an office with a view of the next high-rise? Maybe some stiff-assed boyfriend with about as much guts as a worm?"

"That coffee is for lunch." She snatched the cup from his hand.

"Fine. Maybe it's time I hit some of Jack's twelve-year-old Scotch."

He started toward the dining room, but she dashed to block his way.

"Oh, no, you don't! I won't have whiskey on your breath when the lawyer arrives."

"Stop giving orders." His eyes glinted gold fire. "You don't own this place yet."

"Technically, no, but actually, yes. Watch it, Mister God's Gift to Women, or I'll fire you here and now!" She was on tiptoes trying to get face to face with him as she sputtered out her threat, and suddenly he burst out laughing.

"You do that," he chuckled finally. "You just do that, boss lady. There're guests arriving in two weeks, and you haven't one sweet clue how to deal with them."

Before she could catch her breath, he caught her by the shoulders, pulled her close and brought his mouth down over hers in a mouth-consuming, breathtaking kiss. Drawn full length against his body so fast she didn't have time to conjure a response, her instincts took over...and she kissed him back, full mouth, tongue to tongue.

"Vehicle." He pushed her out at arms' length, head tilted, listening. "Probably the lawyer."

He turned and strode out to meet the newcomer. As the door slammed shut behind him, Allison collapsed against a counter.

Wow! Oh, good lord, no! Not wow. Definitely not wow.

****

Matthew Chamberlain was a tall, handsome, gray-haired man, well groomed and professional. He took the place Allison indicated at the head of the dining room table, declined the sandwiches, accepted a cup of black coffee, then opened his brief case and took out his reading glasses.

As the attorney began to sort through the papers inside his satchel, Allison, seated on his right, took the opportunity to narrow her eyes and purse her lips at Heath, seated across from her. He responded with a syrupy smile that made her blood pressure surge.

"Ah, here it is." Matthew Chamberlain drew out a document and opened it on the table. "There is, of course, the usual sound mind, etc., preamble, which I'm sure you're both familiar with and so I'll leave it unread. Then Jack—Mr. Adams—goes on to mention a particular salmon rod, one with some special significance to you, I believe, Mr. Oakes." He paused and looked at Heath over his glasses.

"Yes." He leaned back in his chair, looking smugly vindicated.

"Well, it's yours."

Allison stifled a sigh of relief. The rest of the estate would be her mother's inheritance.

"Now, here it gets a bit involved." The lawyer settled deeper into his chair and adjusted his glasses. "Mr. Adams was adamant that his real estate, namely this area known as the Chance, be maintained as pristine wilderness and an educational area to enlighten future generations to the need for preservation of it and all places like it. As well..." Matthew Chamberlain raised his gaze from the papers and looked sharply at

57

first Heath and then Allison.

Yes, yes, go on! Get to the point.

"Mr. Adams wanted the Chance to remain in his family in perpetuity. With this in mind, he left forty-nine percent to his granddaughter, Allison Armstrong, and…"

"Fifty-one percent to his daughter, Myra," Allison finished and leaned back in her chair, lips drawn firmly into a smug smile.

"Good." Heath started to rise. "I know Myra will do the right thing by this place."

"A moment, please." The lawyer gestured Heath back into his chair. "You're both mistaken. Mr. Adams did not leave the remaining fifty-one percent to Mrs. Armstrong."

"What? But you said he wanted the Chance to stay in the family!"

"And, according to his thinking, it will, Ms. Armstrong." The attorney glanced briefly over at her before turning to Heath. "He left another forty-nine percent to his acquired son, Heath Oakes."

"Acquired son?" Allison was on her feet, her breath coming in outraged, incredulous gasps. "What in hell does that mean? You can acquire a new dress, or a new car, but not a son!"

"It's merely the adjective Jack Adams chose to explain his relationship with Mr. Oakes." Matthew Chamberlain remained unruffled. "He never legally adopted him, but he'd come to regard him as his own child."

"I don't believe it! Gramps must have been ill or on medication when he made that will. Otherwise, he'd never have left almost half of the place he cherished to

58

a…a jailbird!"

She was on her feet, leaning across the table toward Heath who'd remained stone silent since the announcement of his inheritance.

"If you're referring to Mr. Oakes' past…er… unfortunate brush with the law, I can assure you Jack was convinced nothing of that nature would ever again occur."

"Well, I'm not. I don't even know what he did. He could have robbed or pillaged or raped or…"

"I stole a car." Heath cut off her ranting.

The hint of a smile tugging at the corners of his mouth further infuriated her. Plopping herself back down into her chair, she crossed her arms on her chest with such violence she felt the shoulder seams at the back of her shrunken jacket rip.

"If you'd care to proceed, Mr. Chamberlain, I believe Ms. Armstrong is prepared to listen." Heath's smile turned condescending. "Although she seems to have ignored the fact—or perhaps is not yet aware of it—there remains an outstanding two percent of ownership, which is all important when you consider they hold the balance of power."

Of course! That two percent belongs to Mom. The Armstrongs are back in the driver's seat! She shot him what she hoped was her most triumphant look.

"This is where the will becomes…ah…shall we say, a bit original." Matthew Chamberlain looked from one to the other over his glasses.

"Original? What do you mean, original?" Allison was leaning toward him, hands gripping the edge of the table. "Those controlling shares have to belong to my mother."

59

"Actually, no." The attorney returned his attention to his papers. "They were left in a trust, to be administered jointly by its members."

"A trust? Members? What members? Who?"

"That I can't tell you, Ms. Armstrong. Mr. Adams made the concealment of their identities a top priority. Oh, and there is another stipulation. No one of the property holders can sell their shares unless all parties are in agreement. Now, if you'll both just sign here where it states that you've heard and understand…"

He slid the sheaf of papers toward Allison, indicated where she was to sign, and offered her his pen.

"I'm not signing anything until I have my corporate lawyer examine the document." Allison stood and put her hands on her hips.

"Ms. Anderson, I assure you it's all perfectly legal and unshakeable." Matthew Chamberlain, QC, got up to face her. "Jack Adams spent time and effort making this will. It's one of the most ironclad I've ever encountered."

"Nevertheless, I insist on further legal advice."

"Very well." The lawyer gave an exasperated sigh and began to gather up his papers. "You can pick up a copy from my office when you come into town. I'll have my secretary prepare one for you."

"Thank you." She glanced defiantly over at Heath. The calm coolness on his handsome, sun-bronzed face made her hate him even more.

Five minutes later, Allison watched as Matthew Chamberlain got into his rented Tracker and drove away.

"Seems we finally have something in common."

Heath turned from watching the lawyer out of sight and looked up at her.

She stood on the top step of the Lodge's back porch, leaning against the door, her hands clasped behind her, her head thrown back so that she gazed skyward.

"There has to be a mistake. Gramps would never do anything this crazy."

"It's what he wanted, and we owe it to him to try to make it work."

"Maybe you owe him. I certainly don't!"

She whirled and would have strode into the Lodge had he not bounded catlike up the steps and seized her arm. He spun her to face him, eyes narrowed.

"Oh, yes, you do, Miss High-and-Mighty! You owe him for years of neglect and loneliness. Jack understood the reason for your mother's absences—her fundraising for needy sick kids—and he was proud of her. But you! You had lots of time for vacations at all the holiday hot spots. He showed me the postcards. But not a single day to visit your grandfather. There's no excuse good enough for what you did."

"Let me go! Don't you dare try to heap guilt on me. Not when you're responsible. Not when you were the last one to see him alive!"

"Oh, so we're back to that, are we?" Their faces were inches apart as they stood glaring at each other against the kitchen door. "I suppose the will further strengthens my culpability as a murder suspect, does it?"

"Your vocabulary may have gotten better, but not your manners," she shot back. "I'm catching the afternoon plane to Toronto. My corporate lawyer will have this mess straightened out by the weekend. My mother will own this place, lock, stock, and barrel, and you'll be out on the street!"

She shrugged free of his restraining hand, yanked open the screen door, all but knocking him off the step, and strode into the Lodge.

****

What was he going to do about her? Heath stood on the back steps and drew a deep breath. That will had landed him and her in a fine mess. Bound like Siamese twins in ownership of the Chance, they'd have to find some way to coexist until they discovered who held that powerful two percent. Then, and only then, could they begin to resolve the situation.

Too bad it had to be her entangled with him. She hadn't changed. She was still one stuck-up rich girl with no appreciation of this place Jack Adams had taught him to love and respect. And the way she'd treated Jack all those years, refusing to visit him, leaving him alone after his wife had died... Heartless little bitch.

Loosening his tie and yanking it off over his head, he strode toward his cabin. Who had he been trying to impress by wearing this stupid monkey suit? Had he been stupid enough to think he could throw her for a loop by showing her he could look as sharp as any of those corporate types she worked with at the supposedly impressive job in the city?

Hell! I'm not some city dude. I could see the contempt in her eyes when she looked at me at the church. I dressed for the funeral in remembrance of Jack and the good times. He wouldn't have recognized me in this getup. Damn it, he'd be laughing if he could

62

see me now.

He took the steps to his home two at a time and strode inside. The homey ambience of the place had a calming effect. He removed his jacket and let the peace of the small kitchen restore his equilibrium. What did it matter what he'd done, what he wore? In a few hours she'd be on a plane back to Toronto. With any luck, the lawyers would handle everything, and he'd never have to see her again.

He went into his bedroom, pulled off his clothes, hung his suit in the closet, and headed into the bathroom. He'd showered that morning, but the encounter with Matthew Chamberlain and Allison had left him hot and sticky.

As the water gushed over him, he tried to keep the thought of her as a royal pain, as a burr in his side, but the image of her in those stupid pink pajamas flooded across his mind, and he couldn't suppress the smile that tugged at his lips. Another image formed and more than his lips reacted. The image of her in his arms, the sensation of her lips, her body molding into his…

She's a miserable, money-grubbing little witch. Don't go getting hot after her. That would be just plain stupid.

His body didn't listen. It had a mind of its own where beautiful, sexy Allison Armstrong was concerned. And he hated it.

He was pulling on his bush pants when a knock sounded at his door.

"Heath?" *Damn it, what now?*

"Yeah?"

"I'm ready."

"Ready?"

"To go to the airport. You have to drive me. Well, that is, unless you want me to take the Cherokee and leave it there for you to pick up...which would be difficult since then you'd have two vehicles in town..."

"Okay, okay, I'm coming." He pulled a clean white T-shirt over his head and grabbed a plaid shirt from the closet. *Man, I'll be glad when she's gone.*

In the kitchen, she stood by the door in a shaft of afternoon sunlight and a soft orange turtleneck that accentuated her peaches-and-cream complexion and the soft, shining, artistic tangle of her chestnut curls. Some brand of expensive, hip-hugging jeans highlighted the alluring curves below. *Oh, hell, and double hell. Body behave...just for another hour or so.*

****

"Do you date much?"

"What?" His head jerked to face her. They were driving down the highway toward the airport a half hour later when she broke the silence they'd maintained all the way from the Chance.

"I asked if you date much. Women must be pretty scarce, away back in the woods. Available women, that is." He caught the innuendo.

"I don't fool around with guests, married or otherwise." He returned his attention to the road and fought to control the annoyance that had formed a sharper retort. "Don't try to be subtle about asking."

"What about the local ladies?" Head held high and slightly cocked, she stared through the windshield into the spring sunlight.

"I don't see how my social life is any concern of yours." He gripped the wheel until his knuckles were hard as walnuts.

"I guess it isn't, not really. I'm just curious to see if you'll be leaving any romantic interest when I terminate your position. Or maybe you'll stay in Portage and get a job cutting timber or guiding hunters."

"You're really trying to get to me, are you?" He tried to ignore the anger swelling in his gut. "You hate me that much?"

"That much." She swung to face him, and he saw fury snapping from eyes as green as the burgeoning leaves at the Chance.

"Okay, fine." He turned the Cherokee into the parking lot of the small airport, where a commuter plane was warming up on the runway. "Seems like we've made it." He swung to a stop at the terminal doors and got out, his rapid strides to the back of the vehicle punctuating his annoyance.

"Here." He plunked her suitcase at the entrance. "Safe journey."

With a plethora of feelings roiling in his gut, he climbed back into the Jeep and gunned back toward the highway. He had to find some way to get that irritating woman out from under his skin.

Wonder what Jesse is doing for dinner tonight?

He swung the Jeep into the parking lot beside the former Victorian lumber baron's house that now served at the town's clinic and emergency hospital. Climbing out, he grinned as he read the sign: Dr. Jessica Henderson, MD. *Yeah, that's just what I need...an evening with the good doctor.*

"Heath." The silver-haired receptionist rose to greet him as he entered the foyer that had been converted into a now-empty waiting room. "It's so good to see you. How have you been?" She lowered her

65

tone over the last sentence. "You must miss Jack. I saw you at the funeral yesterday but didn't get an opportunity to talk to you or his daughter. The chestnut-haired girl in the black suit must have been Jack's granddaughter. My, she's grown into quite a lady…a big-city lady, that is."

Heath caught the note of deprecation in her last sentence and had to hold back a grin. He knew Mrs. Henderson had hopes for her own daughter and him. She wouldn't welcome anyone who might push that dream any further from reality.

"She is that. Big city, that is. I just put her on a plane back to Toronto. Is Jesse busy?"

"No, no, finished with the last patient before you came in." The alacrity in her tone upped immediately. "Wait here. I'll fetch her."

Heath let the grin come as she bustled into the office behind her desk. Some day he and Jesse would have to tell her the truth about their relationship. Man, he wasn't looking forward to that day. Somehow he couldn't see Mrs. Henderson accepting the friends-with-benefits thing.

****

"So she's on her way back to Toronto to see if her lawyers can screw you out of your share of the Chance." Doctor Jessica Henderson replaced her wine glass on the table and looked over at Heath. They were seated in Douglas O'Brien's restaurant, the only eatery in Portage other than a couple of fast-food outlets. A candle cast shadows over the couple in the room bathed in twilight and the scent of freshly baked bread and apple pies.

"I guess." He shrugged as he reached for his beer.

"Heath, you can't let her do it." A strong, slender hand reached to cover his on the bottle. "You love that place. Jack loved that place. You owe it to both of you to fight back."

"How?" He looked over at her.

"Get your own lawyer." He saw the blaze in her brown eyes, *Man, she was beautiful.*

"If you hadn't become a doctor, you could have been a model, or an actress, or…"

"Stop avoiding the subject." She pulled her hand away and glared at him. "One of your most attractive character traits has always been your determination to keep Jack's dream alive at the Chance. I'm not about to let you lose it simply because some Toronto businesswoman decides to give you a run for your rights."

"I like it when you have fire in your eyes." His lips quirked up on one corner. "Okay, I'll give it a fight. But lawyers cost big bucks. Jack paid me a decent wage, but I didn't get rich. The bit I put aside is for my mother's retirement. I can't go risking it on the outside chance I might win in a civil case against someone with the connections Allison Armstrong must have."

"I can help." She spoke softly, carefully. "If it's only money that's holding you back…"

"Hell, Jesse, as if I'd take money from you!"

"Okay, okay. Just something I wanted to throw out there. No need to take major offense."

"Sorry." He returned his attention to his beer.

"She's still getting to you…even after more than twelve years." He looked up to see her dark eyes, serious and insightful. "My God, Heath, a girl you fell in love with all that long ago…"

"I never said I fell in love with her." The words snapped out sharper than he'd intended. "Sorry, again." He moderated his tone. "It was a teenage thing that she killed with her spoiled brat persona. Love? I hardly think so. I'd say a lingering animosity is more descriptive of our relationship."

"Really?" Her fingers toyed with the stem of her wine glass as she gazed down into the Chardonnay. "Hmm."

"What's that supposed to mean?"

"Just hmm. Wondering, speculating."

"Well, then, don't. We're out to enjoy the evening."

"And maybe back to my place afterwards?"

****

He paused at the door of her house as she fumbled for the key in her purse. They'd done this many times over the years, when they both needed to share a night without commitment or morning-after guilt. She had no desire to be tied to anyone or anything aside from her medical practice, and he for some reason had never been able to get seriously involved with anyone or anything outside of the Chance.

He watched as she fitted the key in the lock, shoved open the door, clicked on the foyer light, and turned back to face him, smiling. "Well?" She held out a hand.

"Hell, Jesse…" He was stumbling, as awkward as he'd been on that rotten high school date all those years ago.

"Oh, my God. Don't tell me. She comes back after all these years, gives you one hell of a hard time, and now we can't be friends with benefits anymore."

Clamping her hands on her hips, she stared out at him.

"No, no, it's nothing like that. I'm just not…"

"In the mood, have a headache, need to get up early? Come on, Heath, spit out all the old clichés."

"Jesse…"

"What am I saying?" Her words softened as she stepped back outside to stand on tiptoe and kiss his cheek. "I knew this day was coming. The day when she'd either return or you'd really and truly fall in love with someone. Not to worry, my darling. I understand."

She turned, went inside, and closed the door. He stood on the step for a few moments. When she snapped off the porch light, he headed back to his Jeep.

Man, you're an idiot. A gorgeous woman is willing to go to bed with you, and you blow it. That snotty little brown-haired wench from Toronto has done one hell of a job on you. You'd better get over it, and fast.

Chapter Six

Allison turned left, then right. Finally she swung all the way around and glanced back over her shoulder at her reflection in the full-length mirror of her bedroom in her parents' house, the room she'd had growing up, the one she now slept in during visits such as this. She'd decided to stop off to talk with her mother before returning to her apartment, before consulting her lawyer. Her mother always seemed to have a handle on every situation, no matter how difficult. Furthermore, she remembered she'd promised to attend a hospital fundraiser sponsored by her mother's committee.

A smile tipping her lips, she swung around once more. *Yes, there was definitely something to be said for the simple little black dress.*

"What do you think, Jack?" She addressed her mother's standard poodle where he lounged on her bed. Myra had objected to having the dog trimmed into any traditional poodle fashion. He had a full coat of pure white. If he hadn't been kept in shape by proper diet and exercise, he might have looked like a large cotton ball. As it was, he was slim and trim, a prime example of his breed. At Allison's words, he bolted alert and gave a sharp bark.

"You approve? Good. First male opinion of the evening."

She adjusted one of the spaghetti straps over her

bare shoulder, patted the artistic tangle of curls that had taken Gino, her hair stylist, two hours to concoct, and wished Heath could see her now. He'd be at a definite disadvantage in his bush pants and plaid shirt. Lord, she hated that man. She couldn't wait for her father's lawyer to obliterate that will. She'd send him packing so fast it would make his head spin, Snowy River hat and all. She'd tried to begin discussions of the situation with her parents on her arrival, but she'd barely had time to outline the conditions of the will when her mother insisted it was time to get ready for the benefit.

"We'll discuss it in the morning, honey," she'd said.

"Allison, are your ready? Your father and I have to leave soon."

Her mother's voice from downstairs brought her back to the moment.

"Coming," she called, checking her pearl earrings and realizing how well they set off her creamy complexion. She snatched up a black evening jacket and handbag from her bed and hurried downstairs, Jack at her heels.

"Wow, Mom, you look terrific." Allison's tone reflected the sincerity of her admiration when she saw her mother in a floor-length, long-sleeved gown of electric blue, her golden hair elegantly drawn into an upswept style.

"Doesn't she?" Allison's six-foot-tall father, looking the epitome of sophistication in his excellently tailored tuxedo, chestnut hair touched with gray at the temples, beamed down on his wife. "She'll have every man at this barn dance grabbing their checkbook and giving to those sick kids till it hurts. Her daughter doesn't look too shabby, either."

He turned his attention to Allison and grinned broadly, cowboy roots showing through the veneer of big city surgeon.

"That's enough flattery, you two." Myra smiled at the pair. "Allison, I am pleased you agreed to attend this fundraiser with us. We don't spend nearly enough time together as a family."

Oh, God, Mom, don't you start on the family neglect bit. It's bad enough I have Gramps' version of the last original woodsman on my back.

The doorbell rang. Jack gave a sharp bark.

"Who can that be?" Cameron Armstrong frowned as he turned to answer it. "We've got to get going."

"I made it." Paul Bradley's voice gave Allison a start. "Hi, Cam, Myra."

Dressed in a tux, blond hair bright from salon care, he stepped into the foyer and flashed a smile lined with perfectly bonded white teeth and accentuated by what Allison knew, in Canada, in May, on an indoorsy investment banker, had to be a salon-induced tan.

"Made it?" Allison felt she'd missed a beat. A chafe of annoyance washed over her.

"Come on, Al. Don't pretend you've forgotten. I told you I'd take you to your mother's fundraiser if I could get away. And here I am."

Jack muttered a deep-throated growl.

"Stay away from me, you furball," he ordered the dog. "This is a new tux. I don't want it despoiled with your sheddings."

He crossed the entrance hallway to kiss Allison lightly on the lips.

"He's a poodle." She ignored his attempt to draw

Rogue's Revenge

her into something intimate and shrugged away. "Poodles don't shed."

Her words brought a quick response. "I'm not into animals. Can't abide their filthy ways."

"Well, we're delighted you've come," Myra, always the gracious hostess, interjected. "You two can do me a favor. I'll be grateful if you will pick up another case of Champagne at the Lakeside Liquor Store. I don't have time. I have to be at the club to greet the guests. You can take a shortcut through the lane that runs along the greenbelt behind Lakeside Drive. The road isn't paved, but you should still arrive in time for my opening remarks. Believe me, I need all the sympathetic faces I can get in the audience tonight. This is the biggest money raiser of the year. I have to be at my persuasive best."

"Normally, I'd be glad to." Paul turned to Myra. "But I came by cab. I just flew in from Vancouver and haven't had time to get my BMW out of the garage."

"We'll take my car." Allison struggled to keep an exasperated sigh out of her voice.

"Well, that solves one problem." Paul took Allison's arm possessively. "But I'm not sure about the wine. This is a new tux, and those cases can be dirty."

"Here." Cameron Armstrong reached into the closet near the door and pulled out one of his white lab coats. His tone reflected the exasperation his daughter had suppressed. "You can cover it with this."

"Sure…sure…no problem." Paul gingerly accepted the smock. "Let's go, Al. It's starting to rain and, like I said, this is a new tux."

"Good Lord!" Allison breathed as she started her car two minutes later and swung it around the circular

73

drive toward the street. "You'd have thought Mom asked you to bury her father, not just pick up a case of wine."

"What are you talking about?" Paul looked over at her. "Your mother wouldn't ask me to do a thing like that. What's wrong with you, Al? God, you're irritable. PMS or something? I thought you'd be glad to see me. It's been nearly two weeks."

"I'm sorry." Allison braked before turning out onto the tree-lined avenue. She looked over at him and forced a smile. "I've got a lot on my mind. Let's start over and concentrate on having fun tonight, okay?"

They had picked up the wine and were on their way to the country club through Myra's suggested shortcut twenty minutes later when a ragged bolt of lightning rent the black night sky, freeing a downpour.

"Want me to drive?" Paul asked as the car slid in the mud of the dirt road.

"I'm fine, thanks."

"Al, let's stop for a few minutes. It's private out here, and I haven't seen you alone in a fortnight."

"I'd rather not, Paul. Mom and Dad are waiting."

"Ah, come on, Al. They know you're in good hands. Pull over...here."

He grabbed the wheel. Allison yanked back. The car skidded and lurched into a shallow ditch.

"Oh, great!" Allison stared out at the beams of her headlights shining into the trees, reversed, spun tires, and gave up. "We'll never get out of here without a tow."

"So use your cell. While we're waiting to be rescued, we can do some serious making out."

"I didn't bring my phone." She shrugged off his

attempted embrace. "What about you?"

"In the pants I wore on the flight. Didn't think I'd need it tonight."

"Okay, fine. One of us will have to go for help. The club can't be more than a quarter mile ahead."

"One of us!" He sat bolt upright to stare at her. "Well, not me! This is a…"

"I know, I know," she muttered. "A new tux."

She cracked the trunk, pulled the keys from the ignition, and started to get out into the pouring rain.

"What do you think you're doing?" He grabbed her arm.

"Going for help." She shrugged away from him, then swung back to face him. "I have a poncho in the trunk. Lock the doors once I'm gone. I wouldn't want anything to happen to you…or your tux."

****

She was trying to resuscitate Gino's hairstyle in the ladies' room at the country club an hour later when Candace Breckenridge joined her.

"I heard about your little adventure." The older woman, in an elegant ankle-length white sheath, moved to the mirror beside her and patted her hair. "Apparently Paul wasn't up to rescuing a lady in distress. Now if that sinfully sexy camp foreman of your grandfather's had been with you, it would have been an entirely different story, wouldn't it? He wasted no time rescuing me when I had that distressing little incident up at the Lodge on our last vacation. There's a man who knows what to do…both during and after a crisis…especially after, if you know what I mean." She dropped a false-eyelashed lid in a slow wink. "But then, I assume you discovered that fact while you were up

75

there *alone* with him last week?" Her eyes narrowed, her lips pressed into a smile that was more like a smirk.

"That's really none of your business." Allison swung and left the room with as much haughty dignity as she could muster in mud-stained evening shoes and torn pantyhose.

Why did I react like that? I should have calmly denied it. Instead, I left it wide open to speculation. Fool! Now she probably sees me as her competition.

As she returned to the table where Paul and her parents sat, annoyance and disgust colored her mood. It was all Heath Oakes' fault. He was responsible for her irritability with Paul, her repulsion of his attention, her mishap with the car, and now her rude run-in with her mother's friend who, together with her husband, were expected to be major contributors to her mother's charities.

Retaking her seat, she saw Candace Breckenridge standing in front of her husband across the room, her face distorted with anger. From the way she was flailing her arms and gesturing toward the entrance, Allison deduced the woman was demanding to leave.

Robert Breckenridge made futile efforts to calm his wife. Finally he shrugged and took her arm. She slapped his hand away and strode from the room alone. Her husband hesitated; then, with a shake of his head, he followed her.

"Oh, dear!" Myra Armstrong had also witnessed the confrontation. "Robert and Candace must have had another fight. They're leaving, and they haven't made their contribution yet."

Oh, God, not more guilt. I didn't mean to drive them away. A sinking feeling rose in Allison's stomach.

No, not my fault. She revived. *Heath Oakes' fault. The man taints everything he touches, and that includes Candace Breckenridge.*

"I wish I could say I feel sorry for them." Cameron Armstrong shook his head. "Hell of their own making, though."

"Cam, watch your language." His wife laid a restraining hand on his arm. "You're not herding cows on an Alberta ranch now."

"Sorry, darlin', but that pair…"

"What do you mean, hell of their own making?" Allison broke in.

"Now see what you've done." Myra frowned at her husband. "There's no need to go spreading stories."

"Why shouldn't Allison know the truth? Everyone else east of the Rockies seems to. And since Allison is almost half owner of the Lodge that's one of their favorite vacation spots, she should be aware of their situation before she's confronted with it."

"Very well," Myra sighed. "It's such a sad, hopeless affair."

"Sad? Hopeless?" Allison glanced from one parent to another, astonished. "But they're wealthy, socially prominent…"

"Not always the stuff happiness is made of." Dr. Armstrong made a move to tuck his napkin into the neckline of his evening shirt, but his wife's hand stopped him.

"Cam, really. I thought by now you'd have developed decent table manners."

"Just teasin', darlin'." His grin confirmed his words as he chucked her under the chin. "Checkin' to see if you were on your toes."

"Of course." Allison caught the glint of humor in her mother's eyes while the remainder of her expression fought to display exasperation. *Lord, how they love each other; what a wonderful time they have together.* She glanced over at Paul, who'd arrived bone dry in the tow truck sent to his rescue while she was in the washroom. *I wonder...*

"You see, theirs was an arranged marriage of mutual convenience...or so it seemed." Her father's words drew her out of speculation. "When Candace's father, Abe Maxler, became ill many years ago, he started looking around for someone to succeed him as CEO of his multi-faceted company. He knew Candace, his only child, had neither the intellect nor the inclination to do it. But he wanted the firm to remain in the family.

"He saw only one solution. Marry Candace off to an excellent businessman and make him CEO, with the clause that if he ever left Candace he'd face instant dismissal. If Candace left him, she'd be disinherited."

"That's medieval!" Allison couldn't believe what her father was telling her. "I thought that type of thing disappeared centuries ago. No wonder Candace is so..." She stopped, discarded "promiscuous," and opted for "discontent."

"Hang on, hon," Paul admonished. "It's not a crime to marry well. In fact, business these days demands a good appearance on all fronts, personal as well as professional."

"There's nothing wrong with marrying well, of course." Myra, always the peacemaker, stepped in as Allison opened her mouth to respond. "But love and happiness must always take precedence. Otherwise, discontent sets in and…"

"And when a woman who's been unfulfilled emotionally as well as physically in her marriage reaches Candace's age, that discontent can manifest itself in some pretty bizarre behavior." Cameron Armstrong made a display of trying to find the correct fork for the lobster. "Believe me, I saw the problem more times than I care to recall when I was a GP."

"Cam…" Myra reached to hand him the proper utensil, but he caught her slender hand and drew it, palm up, to his lips in a slow, sensuous gesture.

"Okay, sweetheart. I'll behave," he murmured. "Sorry if this old cowboy got out of hand. Forgive me?"

"Always," she breathed, and the light in her mother's eyes told Allison Myra Armstrong definitely wasn't one of those women to whom her father referred.

She was glad her parents weren't like Candace and her husband. The Breckenridges were a deeply troubled couple, and Heath Oakes wasn't making it any easier for them. That womanizing barbarian was a major factor in their problems as well as her own. But not for long. She turned to Paul and smiled.

"Let's dance," she said.

It's a waltz. Take advantage of it, Paul. Hold me close, whisper sweet nothings in my ear. Blast that woods-hero clone out of my mind once and for all.

"Your wish is my command." Paul stood and swept her a mock bow. "Excuse us, Cam, Myra."

He drew her into his arms. "Now, this is more like it," he breathed, moving her about the dance floor in time to the music. "Nothing like a little slow dancing to soothe the savage beast. Or was that savage breast? I never was very good at romantic literature."

"Breast." Allison nestled against him and tried not to let the scent of his three-hundred-dollars-a-tiny-bottle aftershave rankle her. Some day she would have to find a subtle way to tell him she detested it.

"Paul?" She smiled at him, hoping he'd take the hint, hoping he'd recognize that she was searching for romance.

"Ummmm? Hey, hon, isn't that Harrison Graves over there? He's CEO of that new brewery…big bucks. I wonder if he's interested in investing. Follow my lead. I'll dance us over there. Maybe I can bump you into him…get his attention. Look pretty. Smile. This could be a big one."

****

"Damn!"

Allison looked down at the slack left front tire of her car and breathed the curse.

"Allison, please." Her mother, standing beside her in the club parking lot, cautioned, "Remember where you are." She glanced around at guests leaving the facility. "Remember you're a lady."

"Sorry, Mom. It's so damned—darned— exasperating. I thought roadside assistance would have checked for damage before they left it."

"Not a big deal." Her father put an arm around her shoulders. "You can ride home with us. Your mother said you plan to stay the night and discuss lodge business in the morning."

"Good idea." Her father's plan had more than one advantage. "We can drop Paul at his apartment." She ignored the head-shaking grimace he was favoring her with behind her parents' backs. "I'm sure he's tired.

He's been trying to sew up a big business deal with Harrison Graves most of the night."

"Al…" He began the protest, but she silenced him with a finger to his lips and a sly smile.

"I'm taking a few days off to settle Gramps' will, but I won't have to spend my nights with lawyers. We'll have time—lots of time—alone together."

"Well, okay. Promise?"

"I said we will, okay?" Something inside her snapped at his prodding. "Don't push."

"Geez, Al. You've really got a bad case of the crankies or something. Whatever it is, I hope you get rid of it soon."

"Don't worry, I will," she muttered, thinking of Heath. That night she dreamed of a tall, dark, handsome savage in a loincloth.

The next morning she got up early, dressed in her riding habit, and hurried downstairs to find her father finishing his breakfast of coffee, juice, and cereal.

"Your mother and Jack are still sleeping," he greeted her, with one of his wide, cowboy grins. "She worked that room real hard last night. I see you're going riding. How's that mare of yours? I've got to get out there one day soon to see the fine filly she gave birth to…when was it…couple of months ago?"

"Mother and baby are both doing spectacular, thanks for asking." Allison poured herself a cup of coffee and sat down at the table to smile across at her father. "And, yes, you do have to make time to visit Pride and her baby, little Joy. Dad, honestly, she's so cute, with her little whisk of a tail and that lightning blaze down her face…"

"The love of animals lives on in the Armstrong-

Adams dynasty." He favored her with one of his crooked grins that Allison thought made him look roguishly delightful. "Someday soon I'm going to take a week off and the three of us are going on one heck of a trail ride—tents, camp stove, the works."

"I'm going to hold you to it." She finished her coffee and stood. "Got to go. I want to be back in time to have a long chat with Mom before lunch."

"Hold on just a minute, young lady." Cameron Armstrong stood to tower over her. "No one leaves this house without a good breakfast in their belly." He strode to the cupboard and brought a bowl, glass, and spoon to the table. "Cereal and juice before you hit the trail, my girl."

Fifteen minutes later, Allison climbed into her mother's sports car and took the half-hour drive to the stables where she kept her chestnut hunter. She'd ride Heath Oakes' image right out of her mind, she determined as she swung into the flat English saddle and trotted the long-legged thoroughbred into the arena under the critical eye of Jake Morgan, her instructor.

The lesson didn't go well. She couldn't settle her mind to bring herself into harmony with the mare. She took her over the series of jumps poorly, and she knew it. A second round was no better. Nor was a third.

"Ease up on the reins, Allison. Relax and she'll go easier. She's sensing your tension."

"I've been riding since before I could walk, Jake. I think I know what I'm doing." For the first time in the seven years he'd been her riding instructor, Allison snapped at the tall, gray-haired man. She whirled Pride about and headed back at a jump too fast. The mare struggled to rise over the bars but, off stride and over speed, hit the fragile barrier and sent it scattering.

"Drat!" Allison reined the blowing chestnut to a halt near the fence and adjusted her helmet.

"Not her fault." Jake Morgan came into the ring and took the animal by the bridle. "Time to call it quits, Allison."

"Okay, okay." She swung her leg over the mare's rump, kicked her left foot free of the stirrups, and slid to the ground. She paused to brush a fleck of dust from her navy blazer and adjusted her snowy stock. "The fact that the stables are under renovation is throwing her off. All that hammering, and so many strangers around."

"Well…" Jake rubbed the horse's nose and avoided meeting his student's gaze.

"What?" Allison looked sharply at her middle-aged coach. "Spit it out, Jake. If you think I'm a lousy rider, just tell me."

"You're definitely not a lousy rider, honey." His lean, weathered face mirrored all the uneasiness he was feeling. "You're a very good rider, with a heart of gold and the courage of a lion. English style just isn't your cup of tea, so to speak. I'd suggest you segue into western pleasure and ride like your Dad."

"Western pleasure! You've got to be kidding. You mean with a quarter horse and a stock saddle and jeans and a Stetson and…"

"Don't be so quick to turn up your nose, missy. Your dad was a cowboy before he went to medical school and became a fancy doctor. Or have you forgotten his Alberta roots?" Jake released the girth and pulled the saddle and pad from the horse's back.

"No, I haven't." She looked down at her polished riding boots and remembered how proud she'd always been of her father's rise from son of a struggling rancher to one of Canada's best neurosurgeons.

"Well, then." Jake slid Pride's bridle over her ears and replaced it with a halter and lunge line. "Give this mare to your mother—she's retiring her old Princess this summer—and let me find you a good quarter horse."

"Are you saying my mother is a more sophisticated rider than I am?" Allison watched the big, rugged man as he led the mare to the center of the arena and started her moving in wide circles at the end of the lunge line.

"No, just more suited to English than you'll ever be" He clucked to the horse to keep her moving and cooling. "This pretty lady…" He indicated the mare. "Deserves to be with someone who suits her style."

A shrill cry came from the paddocks behind the stables. The mare pricked her ears and answered with a sharp whinny.

"Baby still not ready to leave her mom?" Allison recognized the interchange.

"Pride's a great mother, but she realizes she has to get back to work." He stopped the mare, who stood with her head high, eyes searching, and handed her lead to Allison. "Her baby just isn't ready to give her up. Put this lady in her stall, honey. I'll be in shortly to rub her down. I want to check on the filly. She can get crazy trying to get back with her mom."

Allison took the rope and headed into the stable. It wasn't renovations or Pride's anxiety over separation from her foal that had ruined Allison's performance. No, no, no. It was her lack of concentration caused by one backwoods barbarian named Heath Oakes and his determination to involve her in her grandfather's business. In her mind, she saw his piercing eyes mocking her, felt his body against hers, his mouth covering hers in the most sensuous kiss she'd ever experienced.

Lost in thought, it was a moment before she became aware of hooves galloping into the barn behind her. The next happened so fast that later she'd have difficulty recalling its sequence. A workman's yell, a crash as the mare reared, slamming into Allison's shoulder, high-pitched equine screams.

Thrown against a stall door, Allison staggered, struggling to remain on her feet. As if in a nightmare she saw Pride snorting and pawing amid a cloud of dust and debris, her filly lying immobile on the cement floor in front of her. A six-foot beam lay across the little animal's shattered head.

"Jake!" she screamed as the stable manager ran into the barn and workmen leaped and tumbled down from scaffolding. "Jake!"

****

"Drink this." Myra Armstrong thrust a steaming cup into Allison's hands.

"What is it?" Wrapped in her favorite old fleece housecoat, she sat in her parents' kitchen and stared down into the light brown liquid.

"Hot, sweet tea. The very best thing for shock." Her mother took the chair across from her at the kitchen table, a frown furrowing her forehead. "Honey, are you sure you don't want me to call your father? He's not operating this morning. You really should have your shoulder examined. And you've had a terrible shock."

"I'll be fine, Mom. Just need a little TLC before I go back to my apartment." She forced a smile, but tears trickled down her cheeks. "Oh, God, it was awful! Pride screaming, little Joy lying there with her head covered in blood…"

"I'm sure it was, sweetheart. I empathize with Pride. I can't imagine anything worse than witnessing the death of your baby." She stood and rounded the table to put an arm around her daughter's drooping shoulders.

"Ouch! Sorry, Mom. A bit tender, but I appreciate the gesture." She sniffed and smiled up at her mother. "Got a tissue?"

"Of course." Myra went to the refrigerator to fetch the box from its top. "Poor Jake. He must be full of self-recrimination, letting that filly get away from him. I'll drive out later and talk to him. I hope I can reassure him it wasn't his fault. And honey, I really think you should stay here tonight. I'd like you to be with your father and me…"

The ringing of the phone broke into her words, and she picked up the receiver from its wall rack by the door.

"Hello. Yes, this is Myra Armstrong. Yes, my family is involved with Chance Lodge. What? Oh, no! When? How badly is he injured?"

"Mom?" Allison was instantly at her mother's elbow. "Who? What…?"

"Of course." Myra waved her to silence as she listened. "Someone will be there within twenty-four hours. Thank you for calling."

"Mom, for God's sake, what?" Allison seized her mother's arm the moment she hung up. "The Lodge, what's happened? Who was that on the phone?"

"That was the doctor in Portage." She turned to her

daughter, her face paling. "That's the town nearest the Lodge."

"Mom, for heaven's sake, I know where it is. What did the doctor say?"

"RCMP received an anonymous tip that there'd been an accident up at the Lodge." She crossed the kitchen to drop into a chair at the table. "When they investigated, they found Heath lying unconscious beside the boathouse, a fallen ladder beside him. At first they thought he'd slipped while fixing the roof, but when he regained consciousness, he claimed he remembered the ladder hitting him across the ankles when he went to stand…hitting him too hard to have been a natural slip."

"A deliberate attack?"

"The police aren't certain. Heath has a concussion, and they think he might be confused, but they're investigating, just in case he's not. Allison…" She turned to her daughter. "Your father can't possibly leave his patients, and I'm at a critical stage with my fundraising. You'll have to go. You'll have to take care of Chance Lodge until Heath is well."

"No, Mom. Definitely no!" Allison went to put her empty cup in the sink. "I love you, and I'd do anything for you…except that. And just now, after all that's happened today…"

"Allison, I know you carry some animosity in your heart toward Heath that you've never chosen to explain, but this is your grandfather's place we're talking about. It needs a caretaker, and right now that has to be you. With Heath recuperating at the clinic in town, there's no one to keep it safe."

"And you seriously think my presence can deter

vandals?"

"Allison, the Lodge has a state-of-the-art security system. It just has to be activated at appropriate times. And then there's food and rooms to get ready…guests in two weeks, Heath told me. Hopefully by that time he will be back on the job and his mother will be home, but until then…"

"How do you expect me take time from my job? I may not be a neurosurgeon or a miracle fundraiser, but my position with the company…"

"Didn't you tell me before we went up to Dad's funeral that you'd hired an assistant who's been working out really well? Well, let him take over for a few days."

"But he's still new at the game…"

"Now, you listen, young lady." Allison was startled by the change in her mother's tone. "This is your family we're talking about. I know whatever Heath did years ago turned at least part of your heart to stone, but it's about time you started reacting with what's left of the soft bit."

She picked up the phone and began to punch in a number.

"What are you doing?" Stymied, Allison stared at her.

"Calling our travel agent. You'll need a ticket to catch a plane out of here tomorrow morning."

"But we haven't had time to discuss that crazy will! I haven't consulted my company attorney!"

"You can contest the will a week, a month, a year from now. But it will be a pointless battle if the Chance is destroyed. Yes, hello. I want an open-ended ticket to Portage, New Brunswick. And a large dog crate."

"There," she said five minutes later as she hung up the phone. "All arranged."

"Mom, I do think this is more than a bit uncaring, expecting me to go up to the Lodge to take over God knows what duties from a man I detest, especially after all that's happened today."

"Especially after what's happened today." She put an arm about her daughter. "Dwelling on what happened to Pride and her little Joy won't help anything. On the other hand, getting involved in the challenges involved in taking care of the Chance will. Now you start packing while I get Jack's things together."

"So that's why you asked for a dog crate. Really, Mom, Jack will only be a nuisance. He's never even been in the woods…at least not that kind of woods. I know you take him with you when you ride the bridle trails out at the stable, but northern New Brunswick wilderness is a long way from carefully groomed paths."

"He'll be fine." She smiled benignly as she pulled a bag of dog food from under a cupboard. "He's proven to be a fine guard around the house. I'll feel much better if you have him with you. Actually, he's nearly as resourceful as his namesake…your grandfather."

****

Going back to the Chance and that miserable man. In the last two days my life has done a complete one-eighty.

She plunked down on the edge of the bed in the pink-and-white room she'd occupied as a child and teenager before going off to college, before she'd become Allison Armstrong, tough business woman.

89

What a romantic I must have been. She looked around at the frills and ruffles and again felt the pain in her chest that her denial of all that was lovely and romantic always caused her. And it was all his fault, all because of him.

She picked up the receiver of the pink princess phone beside the bed and tapped in her office number.

"Millie, this is Allison. Put me through to Andrew Burns, will you?"

It was a moment before the corporate attorney's voice answered.

"Allison, good to hear from you. How are things in the wilds of New Brunswick?"

"Good afternoon, Andrew. Have you finished the work on Gramps' will, the copy I faxed you yesterday?"

"Yes, but I don't think you'll be thrilled with what I've found."

"What? Don't tell me…"

"It's ironclad. One of the tightest documents I've run up against in twenty years of practice. Contesting it would be pointless."

"That can't be. There has to be a loophole in such a bizarre document."

"Surprisingly, no. Your grandfather and his attorney left nothing to chance."

The following morning she watched southern Ontario disappearing beneath a heavy cloud cover. As the plane reached cruising altitude and leveled off, she settled back in her seat to consider her next move.

As much as she disliked the prospect, she'd check on Heath as soon as she arrived in Portage. After all, he was an injured creature. Next she'd determine if she needed a temporary caretaker…if she could find a competent one. And if she couldn't? Stay on and run the place herself until she could come up with some way of ridding herself of her share and make a profit doing it?

She leaned back in the seat, closed her eyes, and tried to unwind. What a rotten week this had turned out to be. First, her grandfather's death, then the terrible accident at the stable, followed by the news of Heath's injury, and finally her lawyer's report that he'd found no way to break the will that bound her to the man Gramps had monikered his acquired son.

Heath. His name echoed around in her head as she drifted into a doze. Suddenly he was with her, holding her, those amazing eyes looking deep into hers with a penetrating intensity…

"Would you like a drink, miss?" The flight attendant interrupted her half-lucid thoughts.

"Yes, please." She jerked upright. "A diet soda. With lots of ice."

Late that afternoon, after the commuter plane had touched down in fog and mist at the small northern New Brunswick airport nearest Chance Lodge, she collected her luggage and Jack. With the dog's leash in one hand and her single suitcase in the other, she hailed a cab.

"Where to, miss?" the driver asked, eyeing the big poodle.

"To the medical clinic."

"I don't usually take dogs. Shed much?"

"Not at all. He's a poodle. Double fare?"

"Climb in."

"You're a liability already, and we've only just

91

arrived," she muttered to the dog as the driver deposited her suitcase in the trunk and she opened the rear door to let the animal inside. With a happy bark, Jack leaped up on the seat and took his place by the opposite window.

"I'd like to see Heath Oakes," she told the receptionist at the front office a few minutes later. "My name is Allison Armstrong. My grandfather owned Chance Lodge."

"He checked himself out early this morning." The gray-haired, middle-aged lady behind the desk surprised her with the reply. "Dr. Henderson tried to convince him he wasn't in any fit condition, but, well, if he works for your family, you must know what he's like. There's no stopping him when he's got his mind set. If Dr. Henderson couldn't convince him to stay in the clinic, no one could. I'm sure they'll be announcing their engagement any day now. And who is this fine fellow?" She turned her attention to the dog and beamed down at him. Jack, tongue lolling happily, looked up at her, bright and pert.

"Nell, what are you gossiping about now?" A brunette with gorgeous violet eyes, porcelain complexion, and shampoo-model hair stood framed in the doorway of an examining room, her white lab coat open to reveal a short, fitted dark skirt, red silk blouse, and legs that seemed yards long in black hose. Allison's heart plummeted.

"Dr. Henderson?" She hoped her voice wasn't squeaky with surprise.

"Yes. You were looking for Heath. I overheard." She crossed the room and extended a cool, slender hand. "I'm Jessica Henderson, his doctor."

"Allison Armstrong." She accepted the

introduction with what she hoped was mature, woman-to-woman cool. "When my mother and I learned he'd been injured, we decided one of us would have to come. How is he, Doctor?"

"Stubborn, tough, and definitely on the mend." She shrugged and smiled ruefully. "I would have preferred his staying here a couple more days until I was sure all was well, but he refused. He had work to do at the Lodge, he said…guests arriving soon, and all that."

She went to a cupboard in one corner of the immaculate room, unlocked it, and took out a bottle of pills.

"I assume you'll be going up to the Chance?" She handed it to Allison. "These are painkillers he should be taking."

"I imagine you'll be coming up soon, too." Allison couldn't resist testing the waters of the relationship the receptionist had mentioned.

"Me? No. Not unless one of you think I'm needed." The doctor looked puzzled. Then her expression cleared, and she chuckled. "Oh, Mom's been airing her wishful thinking again, has she?"

"Now, Jesse, he's a fine man, and you're not getting any younger, and I would like to be a grandmother before I die…"

The receptionist arose and went to put a placating hand on the doctor's arm.

"Mom?" Allison was surprised.

"Meet Nell Henderson, my mother, receptionist, and shameless matchmaker." Jessica Henderson put an arm about the older woman's shoulders and hugged her. "It's fortunate I love her and understand she wants only what she thinks is best for me. You have a mother, Miss

Armstrong. I saw you with her at Jack's funeral. You understand."

"Definitely." Allison pocketed the pills and forced a smile. "Thanks. I'll let you know if Heath needs further medical attention." *Good lord, why did I put emphasis on "medical"?*

Out in the street she saw her cab and hailed it again.

"Chance Lodge, please." She started to put her suitcase into the rear seat, but the driver stopped her.

"Sorry, lady, but I won't take this car up there...not even for a double fare. Only four-wheel-drives on that road."

"Well, then, how am I supposed to get there?"

"You might try renting Jordon Jones' Tracker." He pointed to a service station/convenience store across the street. "He lets it out sometimes."

"Thanks." Allison shut the cab door, hefted her luggage, adjusted her hold on Jack's leash, and headed across the street.

"Good afternoon," she said to the blond teenage clerk behind the counter as she entered the service station's store section. Over in one corner, four local men whose mackinaws, work pants, and steel-toed boots branded them woods workers were gathered around a coffee machine. They stared at her and Jack. One of them pointed at the poodle and snickered.

"What's that? A cotton ball on legs?"

"I'd like to rent a four-wheel-drive." She ignored them and spoke when the girl behind the cash register looked up from the magazine she'd been scanning. "The cabbie said I might be able to get one here."

"We only have one." The teenager snapped her

gum and looked Allison critically up and down. "And it's out right now. Where'd you want to go?"

"Chance Lodge. How long before it gets back?"

"Tomorrow, probably." She shrugged and returned to her reading. "Ben Jenkins never is real exact about when he's coming down out of the woods. Likes to keep his wife guessing."

"I'll drive you up to the Chance."

One of the men moved out of the coffee group and ambled over to her, Styrofoam cup in hand. He was huge and bearded with black whiskers. Equally dark, untidy hair stuck out from beneath a stained baseball cap. Over six feet tall and weighing, Allison estimated, well in excess of two hundred pounds, he was a formidable brute.

"How much?" She looked up into his small, bear-like eyes.

"Forty bucks, take it or leave it. Ten more if you're taking that white thing along. Marty Mason don't dicker."

"Fine. Let's go, Mr. Mason." *What a rip-off, but I have to get there.*

"Hold your horses. I have to gas up first. Darrell, you wanta give me a hand? Wait here, lady. I'll give you the high sign when I'm ready. No need for you to wait out in the cold and damp."

****

"Come on, come on!" He waved impatiently at her through the service station window five minutes later. "I want to get back to town before dark."

Grabbing her suitcase and Jack's leash, she went to join him beside a dented, mud-splattered Jeep.

"That thing..." He jerked a finger at Jack. "And

95

your suitcase in the back."

What happened to the guy who didn't want me waiting in the cold and damp? Allison lowered the tailgate, hefted her suitcase into the rear, and urged Jack into the grungy space beside it. The poodle circled twice before finding a place he deemed decent to plant his bottom. He turned reproachful eyes on Allison.

"I know, I know," she hissed below the hearing of the driver, who was revving the engine. "It's filthy, but it's the best I…we can do." She slammed the dented tailgate back into place and went to the passenger side, glad she'd chosen to dress in jeans, turtleneck, barn coat, and running shoes.

The interior was no better than the exterior. Dirty and reeking of stale smoke, the vehicle had torn upholstery and a dash so smeared and streaked Allison wondered how the man could read the gauges. Dead bugs coating the windshield lowered road visibility. *Don't get picky. It's only a little over a half-hour drive to the Chance. I can tolerate this backwoods creep and his filthy excuse of a vehicle for that long.*

"You're Jack's grandkid, right?" With a grinding of gears, they headed out of the parking area.

"Yes," she replied, trying to keep the stench from unhinging the stomach muscles responsible for keeping her last meal in place.

"Old Jack. Now, there was a character." He chuckled and flashed a grin over nicotine-yellowed teeth. "Real birds-and-bees lover. Wouldn't kill a black fly if it was on the end of his nose. Crazy as a loon, I always said."

"He was a conservationist." Allison forced back a sharp retort. She couldn't quarrel with this man. At least not until he got her to the Chance.

"Yeah, well, that's as may be. But he should have had at least one rifle up at his place, what with all those stories of sasquatch sightings the last year or so."

"Sasquatch sightings! Up at the Chance? You've got to be joking. There are no such creatures. And even if there were, they're supposed to be native to the Pacific Northwest."

"Maybe." Her driver shrugged. "But Jack's business is suffering because of it. Men who used to bring their wives and kids up to the Lodge started coming alone."

"That's crazy!" Allison snapped. "It's just a stupid ghost story."

"Maybe, maybe not." He turned on his headlights as fog began to creep over the road and the mist thickened. "I've seen it myself, and it's something I won't soon forget. I won't go into the woods up there without a rifle while that half-man, half-ape thing is around. No, sir, not me. I tried to tell Heath to be careful, but he wouldn't listen. How is the stubborn bugger, anyway? I heard he had an accident."

"He fell from the boathouse roof," she replied. "According to Dr. Henderson, his injuries are painful but not life threatening."

"Well, good. Him and me, we've had our differences from time to time, but I wouldn't want to see him hurt bad or anything— Sweet merciful heaven, look!"

He braked to a violent stop that sent Allison pitching forward and brought a yike from Jack. Following the direction of the man's stunned stare, Allison caught a glimpse of something large and hairy shambling across the fog-shrouded trail about twenty yards ahead of them. As quickly as it had appeared, it vanished into the trees.

"There! I told you," Marty Mason barked. "Sasquatch. Second time I've seen the hairy bugger. Now maybe you'll believe me." He let off the brake and roared ahead up the trail at such a speed Allison, in spite of her seatbelt, bounced nearly to the roof.

"Hey, slow down." Sasquatch or no sasquatch, she didn't want to be killed when this dirty vehicle left the road and crashed into a tree.

"Not on your life, lady. It's gettin' on to dark, and I want to be back in town before moonrise. I don't relish bein' caught out on this road alone with that critter."

Someone in a Halloween costume. Or a really big black bear, its coat grayed with mist. Both perfectly reasonable explanations. Or were they? With her heart still bumping at her ribs, she knew she'd be glad to get out of this shadowy forest and into the safety of Chance Lodge.

****

Chance Lodge and its grounds appeared deserted when Marty Mason stopped his vehicle in the dooryard. Only the canvas-topped Jeep and the Cherokee parked near Heath's cottage denied the fact.

"I'll be takin' that pay now, miss." He looked over at her, eyes narrowing as he held out a grubby hand.

"Of course." Allison dug into her pocket, pulled out a wallet, and handed him the fare. "Thank you."

A slight sound made her turn toward the storage barn, and she saw him. Watching her from its doorway, one hand above his head gripping the top of the frame, he was a tall, lean outline in the mist.

"Brought you a little something to make you feel better, Heath," Marty Mason hollered out his window as Allison climbed out and headed for the rear of the Jeep. "I'd advise small doses, though. I do believe she's potent stuff."

Allison barely had time to retrieve her suitcase and get Jack to jump out before, with a raucous laugh and grinding of gears, the man swung his vehicle around and headed back down the trail.

"What are you doing here?" Heath asked when the noise had died in the distance. "Managed to break the will or something?" He remained where he was, his tone sardonic.

"No." She held her ground, too, and stayed, suitcase in one hand, Jack's leash in the other, where she was. "Dr. Henderson informed my mother of your accident and she—my mother, that is—decided someone from our family had to come to see if the Lodge needed a temporary caretaker. Dad has a full caseload, and Mom is winding up a major fundraiser. I was the only one *she* saw as being available."

"Myra. I should have guessed."

He dropped his hand and advanced toward her, limping. When he got close enough for her to see his features in the fading light, she gasped.

"My God!"

His left eye was black and swollen, his lower lip split, and his right cheek purpled with bruising. "I had no idea…"

"I've survived worse." He looked down at Jack, his features relaxing into a crooked grin. "Who's this handsome lad?"

"This is Jack." *No snide remark, no cotton ball*

joke. Surprising.

"Hello, Jack." The dog gave a sharp little bark, sat, and held up his paw.

"Nice to meet you, too." He accepted the offer. "Guess you're named after someone pretty special. Come on." He straightened, extended his hand for her suitcase, and grimaced. *Hurting more than he wants anyone to know.*

"Never mind." She pulled it back from him.

"Fine." He turned toward the Lodge, limping. "You don't have to keep that poor guy on a leash up here. Let him stretch his legs. What did you have to do to get Marty Mason to drive the two of you up here?"

"Money convinces."

"Doesn't it always. Come on, Jack," he continued as she released the dog. "I think I have a nice, juicy bone in the refrigerator."

With a joyful bark, the poodle bounded along beside him, apparently delighted with his new friend.

Right. Alienate my dog, why don't you. What great protection he'll be once he's been plied with his favorite food. Hefting her suitcase, Allison followed.

"That man, Marty Mason, didn't seem to be overly fond of Gramps or anything to do with this place. Why?"

They were at the Lodge steps. As he mounted the first one, Heath turned back on her. "Because I fired him a month ago."

"Again, why?" Allison looked up at him.

"He was belligerent and not adhering to our environmental code and goals. Satisfied?" He continued on up the steps and pulled open the door.

"Satisfied." She followed him. "He told me there's

a sasquatch living on the Chance. Actually, we did glimpse something on the road…"

"Yeah, right." Heath's response was a sneer as he stepped aside to let her proceed him inside. "One foolish woman sees something furry in the bush and right away we have a sasquatch. It would have passed like the farce it is if she hadn't spread the story like jam on a hot muffin."

"And that hurt business?"

"What do you think?" He snapped on a light to relieve the twilight gray spreading into the room.

"Do you have guests now?" She set her suitcase to one side and removed her jacket.

"No, not for another ten days. Don't worry. My mother will be back by then, and I'll be able to handle my work."

"Go into the living room and put a match to the fireplace." She wasn't about to let him start hitting her with sentimental junk. "It was always kept ready, and I'm sure you've continued the practice. I'll get food. There must be homemade soup either in the freezer or refrigerator. It used to be a staple here."

"Refrigerator," he said, gingerly removing his plaid mackinaw. "Beef barley. So you do remember some of the traditions."

"Some of them." She pulled the bottle of pills Dr. Henderson had given her from her pocket and handed them to him. "From Dr. Henderson."

He snapped off the cover, shook a few into his hand, and gulped them down.

"Hey, how about reading the directions?"

"He-men don't read instructions." He choked.

"Right. Besides your face…?" Allison headed for

the sink and poured him a glass of water. She tried to keep compassion out of her voice as she got a good look at him in the kitchen light. He'd needed those pills.

"A few bruised ribs, a twisted hip, nothing life threatening." He took the water and swallowed.

"Sit." Allison shoved a kitchen stool over to him.

"What?"

"Sit. I'm going to take your boots off."

"No way. I'm perfectly capable of…"

"Sure you are." Her tone softened. "But it hurts, and there's no need to punish yourself. So let go of that macho pride and sit."

"Okay, okay." He sank back onto the stool. She knelt and began to unlace his left boot.

"This could be a really hot moment, you know."

She looked up and saw a wicked gleam in his eyes.

"Don't get carried away, He-Man Oakes. I've simply got too much of my parents' compassionate blood flowing through my veins to let anyone or anything suffer needlessly."

"And maybe a drop of Jack's?"

"Okay, okay, maybe a drop of Gramps' blood, too." She yanked the boot from his foot and he flinched.

"Ugh."

"Sorry. Stop your guilt tripping and I'll try to be more gentle. Do you have any idea who might have caused your fall?"

"No, but whoever did it never meant to do more than shake me up. Otherwise he could have finished the job while I was out cold."

"He might have killed you with the fall."

"I don't think murder was his intention. Dead, I couldn't sign away my share of the Chance. James

Wilcox is willing to play rough to get what he wants, but I think he'd draw the line at premeditated murder. And so, I think, would you."

"James Wilcox? Me? You can't be serious! This place certainly isn't worth risking a murder charge."

"Interesting. You seemed to think I was willing to give it a try."

"Yes, well, maybe." She finished unlacing his right boot, but this time she eased it from his foot. "The jury is still out on that one."

"Ah, so now there's a jury. I'm not being condemned without a trial. Guess I've moved up a notch in your estimation."

"It had to be a thief or a vandal." She recalled the well-dressed man who had accosted her and her mother at the funeral and found Heath's suspicions farfetched.

"Then why didn't he take anything while I was unconscious?"

"I can't explain that. I only know civilized professional people do not resort to violence as a means to an end. Especially not for a few acres of trees."

"You don't know the facts." Heath got off the stool. When she stood to face him, she discovered that even in his stocking feet he was still a good six inches taller than she.

"What facts?"

"The government has recently put a freeze on the sale of all crown-owned waterfront property along this river." He walked gingerly across the kitchen, then turned to face her, his back to the cupboards. "Only privately owned property can be purchased, and that's subject to a lot of environmental conditions. For example, land already designated for private recreational homes has to stay that way; there can no longer be any reclassification to commercial use. And since this is the only property on the river already with a commercial designation, it's the only one available that can take paying guests. In other words, we're the only game in town."

"But why this river, this lodge? Surely there are others on other rivers…"

"Ah, yes, but not on a river like the North Passage. It's an adventure river, offering everything from great trout and salmon fishing to Class Four rapids for adventurers. Its wildness and inability to be navigated by power boats has kept it pristine, its surrounding wilderness unspoiled. That was why Jack screened his guests so carefully. He didn't object to catch-and-release fishing—it often provided his bread-and-butter crowd—but he did mind hunters and people on ATVs who had no respect for the land and its creatures. He wanted this to be a place people came to enjoy nature and the wilderness, leaving only tracks behind and taking only pictures and great memories away. And," he said heading for the refrigerator. "I intend to see it stays just that way."

He opened the appliance door and took out the largest beef bone Allison thought she'd ever seen.

"Here, buddy. I bet you're hungry." He handed it to the eager dog. "Can't have anyone named Jack uncomfortable in this house."

Chapter Seven

Allison watched Heath go through the swinging door, Jack happily carrying his supper in his jaws at his heels. She shook her head, then turned toward the refrigerator. Stubborn, that's what Heath Oakes was, just plain stubborn.

Ten minutes later she followed, two steaming bowls of soup on a tray in her hands. When he jerked upright as she placed it on the coffee table in front of him, she suspected he'd been dozing. Painkillers kicking in, no doubt. Jack, gnawing contentedly on the huge bone, lay at his feet.

So much for canine loyalty. One tyrannosaurus rex bone and he's anyone's best friend.

"Soup's on." She handed a bowl and spoon to the man coming alert.

"Thanks." He took them from her. "Looks good."

"It's only soup." She sat down on the opposite end of the couch.

"Ambrosia to someone who used to live for days at a time on oatmeal and macaroni."

Bullets of reality, his unexpected words shattered her image of him as always having been a tough, self-reliant street kid.

"You're not serious," she said, staring at him.

"Yeah, well…" He avoided her wide-eyed incredulity. "I guess being cold and hungry just now

105

brought back a lot of 'back in the day' stuff."

"So you became an outlaw...like Robin Hood?" she asked, remembering his innuendoes about an incarceration.

"Always the romantic, aren't you?" He looked over at her, his eyes narrowing to yellow slits in the firelight. "No, I was just a street kid in secondhand clothes, out to make the world sorry it had kicked him in the teeth."

"What did you do?"

"I told you. I stole a car. To top it off, I crashed it into a tree after a high-speed chase by police." He replaced his soup bowl on the tray and hunched his shoulders into a stretch. "They can put you in jail for that kind of thing." He leaned back on the couch and stared into the flames.

"And did they?" *So he had been an outlaw, of sorts.*

"Oh, yeah." He pulled himself to his feet with a grimace and went to put a log on the fire. "They sure did."

"Why would you do anything so foolish?" she asked. "If you felt you had to steal, why not food or clothes or...money? Something you could use?"

"Because I was mad as hell, fed up with never having what all the other kids seemed to take for granted, but mostly because I'd been humiliated by someone I thought really liked me."

"A girl?" Allison asked softly and couldn't help admiring his broad shoulders and narrow hips as he remained hunkered down in front of the fire, watching the new log begin to blaze.

"Yeah, a girl. A snotty rich girl whose homework I did for an entire term because she promised to go to a school dance with me in June."

"And she didn't?"

"She sure didn't." His words were a half caustic laugh, half sneer. "She let me come to her house all dressed up in a secondhand suit my mother had spent her last ten dollars to buy, a bunch of flowers I'd salvaged from a supermarket dumpster in my hand, then greeted me at the door with her real date and a bunch of her rich-kid friends. They were laughing up a storm."

"Oh, my God." The three words came out in a whispered gasp. "What did you do?"

"I did something really smart." Sarcasm colored his words as he stood and turned to face her. "I stole her father's BMW and wrapped it around a tree after a race with the RCMP."

"Heath…" She tried to speak and failed. The image of a tall, gangly teenager in a shabby suit, his hopes and dreams shattered in one heinous moment of senseless cruelty, had formed a massive lump in her throat. "I'm sorry."

"Go to bed. Just go to bed, will you?" His face in the flickering firelight was hard and cold, a twitch afflicting his jaw. "I don't need any rich woman's sympathy. You're all a bunch of bitches."

"Fine. Come along, Jack. We'll leave Nasty Ned alone. He doesn't need our company. I'm sure he'll be able to amuse himself…tarring all financially secure women with the same brush."

The poodle paused, looking up at Heath.

"Go on," he waved a dismissive hand at the dog. "You belong with her."

With a sigh, Jack turned away and followed

Allison to her room.

****

"Coffee?" Allison stepped out onto the front veranda where Heath was replacing a rotted plank, two mugs in her hands. The bright, frosty morning raised steam from the cups and formed a misty barrier between them. Jack, who'd been at her heels, gave a joyful yelp and raced down the steps to run madly around the grounds.

"Thanks." He got up, eyeing her suspiciously as he accepted the mug.

"Beautiful day." She drew a deep breath of the crisp, clear air and savored it. "I'd almost forgotten how terrific early mornings are up here."

"About last night." He stared down into his cup. "I talked too much, courtesy of those painkillers."

"Would you like me to forget it?"

"I'd be grateful." He looked up at her.

"Done. Oh, look! A pair of black ducks. Probably coming to nest."

He grunted and turned away.

"And just what is that supposed to mean?" She caught him by an arm.

"They won't be coming much longer...not if this place is sold to National Realty." He rested his hips against the railing and took a sip of coffee.

"Look, I know how Gramps felt about this place, how you feel about it, but I'm not about to commit myself to a life in the backwoods. I have a job..."

"Yeah, yeah, CFO of some big company, right?" He straightened up, set his coffee on the railing, and knelt to return to his work. "Making money like it was going out of style."

"So what if I am?" she snapped. "You don't know anything about me, about my plans and goals."

"I know they don't include a commitment to Jack's hopes and dreams." He drove a nail into a plank with a mighty blow. "I know you don't give a damn if National Realty buys it for their client and he proceeds to pave these entire grounds with asphalt and puts flashing neon lights over the Lodge."

"That's not true! I do care! But I'm not going to spend the rest of my life trying to prevent it."

"Okay, okay. Just don't expect me to hand over my part of this place without one hell of a fight." He picked up another nail and slammed it into the wood harder than the previous one. The veranda flinched.

"You're on, Wilderness Willy. Be prepared to leave this place with your tail between your legs! Very soon."

She snatched up his cup and strode back into the Lodge.

Jack paused in his cavorting to stare after her. Then his delight in the place resurfaced and he raced off again to play.

A half hour later, the sound of a vehicle made her glance out the kitchen window. He was driving out of the yard in the Cherokee. Going to town? He had to be. Otherwise, he would have used the old Jeep. To meet with a lawyer? Or maybe to see the beautiful Dr. Henderson? She tried to put a quick end to the sinking feeling that came over her at the latter possibility. *Mind over matter*, she told herself sharply. *Just imagine living indefinitely with the creature. That should fix it.*

She rinsed the coffee cups, then wandered about the Lodge, Jack at her heels, as she reacquainted herself with each nook and cranny. Nothing much had changed, she discovered. The same outdoor and wildlife paintings donated by Jack's wealthy guests still adorned the walls of the dining and living rooms; the same dishes and silverware still graced the sideboards and china cabinets, and, to her chagrin, the same feeling of home and hearth and security still prevailed.

I don't belong here, not anymore, not now, not with him, so shelve the sentimental stuff.

She reached the door of her grandparents' apartment. With her hand on the doorknob, she hesitated. This had always been a special place for her as a child, the equivalent of Grandma's house. She felt she couldn't bear it if it had been changed in any way. God forbid it had been made into a storage area for extra furniture. The idea made her shiver. Steeling herself for the worst, she shoved open the door. A wave of relief swept over her. Everything was exactly as she remembered it.

Stepping inside, she felt a rush of nostalgia so powerful it left her lightheaded. She walked softly into the reverend hush, crossing the room to open the curtains on the wide patio doors that led to a deck overlooking the river. A beam of sunshine illuminated the apartment, and in it Allison suddenly saw the image of her grandmother sitting in the big rocker by the window, knitting and looking up to smile fondly at her only grandchild.

"Gram." The word choked as the vision dissolved into dust motes dancing in the radiance.

With a lump rising in her throat, she turned toward the big fourposter bed at the back of the room. Plump with pillows and quilts, it appeared the epitome of warmth and intimacy, a place to share with someone special. How lonely that bed must have been these past ten years for her grandfather.

She moved to the corner fireplace. Its grates had been swept clean, but she could still remember chilly evenings spent before its cheerful blaze.

On the mantel were photos of herself with her parents as a baby, as a child, as a teenager, and as a college graduate. *Gramps loved me, and I wasn't there when he needed me, all because of a barbarian named Heath Oakes.*

Her eyes burned, her throat constricted. *I don't need to load myself down with any more recriminations. Heath Oakes is doing a state-of-the-art job of it.* She sucked in a deep breath. *Moping around here isn't helping. Shopping might help raise my spirits. I'll go to town.*

She looked out the window at the old Jeep sitting alone by the shed. *Well, since there's no choice…Anyhow, if he can drive it, so can I.*

Ten minutes later, struggling to get the knack of driving the ancient standard-transmission vehicle, she was roaring about the Lodge grounds. It bucked and balked and was every bit as trying as a two-year-old colt. But Allison Armstrong had mastered more than one of those in her time. With teeth clenched and lips drawn into a pencil-thin line, she persisted until she felt reasonably in control. Then she headed down the tunnel of greenery toward Portage. She was glad she'd left Jack in the Lodge. In this vehicle, he'd have been bounced more than she cared to think.

At the service station on the edge of the village she noticed the gas gauge was reading empty and the oil light was flashing.

"Fill it up and check the oil, please," she told the attendant, who was appraising her critically. "May I use your phone for a long-distance call? I'll use my card."

"You're Jack's grandkid, aren't you?" he asked. When she nodded, he grinned, "Sure, sure, go right ahead. Anything for Jack's family."

She went inside and told the gum-chewing teenager she had permission to use the phone. Hardly bothering to look up from her magazine, the girl shoved it across the counter toward her.

The place was empty except for the distracted clerk. Allison quickly punched in her parents' number. She preferred to talk to her mother without an audience, and at any minute someone might come in.

Shortly she had Myra on the line and was telling her that Heath appeared perfectly capable of looking after the Chance.

"I'll be on the flight to Ottawa tomorrow afternoon," she concluded.

"So soon?" Myra sounded surprised. "I thought you might like to spend a few days renewing old memories."

"Have you forgotten? I have a job. Anyway, with Heath Oakes as my sole companion, I'm eager to get the heck out of here. See you tomorrow. Love to Dad."

She hung up before her mother could respond, thanked the teenager, who nodded despondently, and headed down Main Street.

The town, she discovered now that she had a chance to see it up close at her leisure, hadn't changed much over the years of her absence. It still consisted of a single main street with a few owner-operated establishments on either side. There was a hardware store, a bakery Allison remembered made the best sticky buns she'd ever tasted, a shoe store, a furniture outlet, a grocery store, a craft boutique, and, across from the village's only restaurant, a shop that sold clothing for the entire family.

Noting the restaurant owner was setting out a couple of sidewalk tables in the spring sunshine, she headed for the clothing store, with a smile. Her grandfather had always said spring had arrived when Douglas O'Brien set up his sidewalk cafe.

As she stepped inside, the bell over the door tinkled. Allison remembered the sound from the days when she, her mother, and her grandmother had shopped there. Nothing else had changed much, either, she realized as she glanced about at the crowded racks of merchandise filling the center area and the carefully piled sweaters and shirts on shelves along the walls.

The narrow strips of hardwood that formed the floor were the same, too, a little worse for wear but still just as much a part of the old store's ambience as its tin filigree ceiling. Only a few posters along the walls, advertising brand-name outdoor wear, appeared new.

A wave of nostalgia swept over her as she remembered a visit to the shop with her grandmother. She recalled Grammie Adams, her blue eyes bright with pleasure, holding the little pair of jeans to her six-year-old granddaughter's waist and declaring them perfect.

"May I help you?"

The saleslady's voice made Allison start. She turned to see Mildred Wilson, the store owner, smiling at her.

"Why, if it isn't little Allison!" Beaming with

delight, the white-haired woman hurried to grasp Allison's hands in hers.

"Hello, Mrs. Wilson." Allison smiled as the familiar scent of the slender, well-groomed woman's lavender perfume brought still more memories rushing back. "How are you?"

"Fine, just fine, honey. My, you're as beautiful as your mother. But that hair and those eyes have to be your father's. Is he still as handsome as ever?"

"Still." Lord, it felt good, this ambience of being welcomed back home, of belonging.

"I'm so sorry about your grandfather." Mildred Wilson became serious. "He was a fine man. His Lodge and its guests were a real boon to this village where there's no industry and most people live by lumbering, farming, or fishing. Oh, we survived before the Chance, and I expect we'll survive again, if…" She paused. She didn't have to finish. Allison got the picture.

"I can't believe Gramps' guests would find much to buy here." Allison gently tried to downplay the Lodge's importance. "Most of those people were a pretty upscale lot."

"That's exactly the point!" Mildred Wilson clapped her nicely manicured, heavily ringed hands. "Some were seasoned outdoors people, but a lot weren't. They frequently arrived here with all the wrong clothes, all the wrong equipment. Why, I finally brought in a whole selection of hiking and recreational clothing, just to fill their needs. Ellis' Hardware sold fishing equipment like you wouldn't believe!"

"Really?" Allison was astonished.

"Definitely. Mary Davis' craft boutique has flourished because of their appetite for handmade quilts, home-knitted sweaters, and authentic wood carvings. Even the service station benefited from those who drove up here, and, would you believe, Douglas O'Brien has actually become famous for his oyster stew!"

"I had no idea the Chance had such a wide-reaching effect on the community," Allison said.

"Well it has…had. Before Jack opened up, we survived. Afterwards, we had a little icing on our cake. Oh, well," she changed the subject as Allison's forehead furrowed. "Enough reminiscing. What can I do for you, honey? Some hiking clothes, maybe?" She looked hopeful.

"Actually what I need is a nice, simple dark suit. Mine got ruined in the rain at Gramps' funeral."

"Dark suit? Hmmmm. Size eight? Ten? Not much call for dark suits in May. Let me look upstairs. Browse around while I'm gone. You might see something else you'd like."

Allison was idly flicking through a rack of Nonfiction sweatshirts when she happened to glance out the front window and saw Heath and Jessica Henderson seated at Douglas O'Brien's newly established sidewalk cafe. The proprietor was standing back, hands on his broad, white-aproned hips, apparently awaiting their opinion on the steaming bowls of food in front of them. His famous oyster stew?

Heath dipped a spoon, raised it to his mouth, tasted, then looked up at the chef with a nod of approval. O'Brien gave a thumbs-up gesture and ambled back inside. As soon as he'd gone, Heath leaned across the table to speak to his companion. His expression told Allison the subject was serious.

At first Jessica appeared to be listening receptively. Then the situation changed. She shook her head vehemently and threw up her hands.

Heath leaned across the table, talking fast, seizing one of her upraised hands. For a few moments she continued to protest, but as he kept up his flow of words, slowly acquiesced. As Allison watched, the doctor's hand fell to the table top, enveloped in his. Something in Allison Armstrong, CFO, sank like a stone. *What can he be saying to her, trying to convince her about?*

He picked up his hat from an empty chair and stood, still holding her hand. Reluctantly, it appeared to Allison, Jessica followed suit. To her dismay, they headed across the street toward the clothing store.

"Mrs. Wilson? I have to leave. I'll try to get back later," she called up the stairway. "Thanks for your help."

She dodged between racks of Levis, past stacks of hiking boots, and through the rear door.

Once outside, she flattened herself against the old building's weathered shingles, then wondered what in the world she was doing. She had every right to be in town, in that store. Why was she hiding? She wasn't afraid to face a man she despised, or his lady friend. She'd march back in there and...

She started to open the door. Through the first few inches she saw Heath holding up a pair of women's bush pants for the doctor's approval. She took them from him and held them to her waist.

Allison eased the door shut. *Planning a camping trip together. Good. That would keep him out of her way.* But as she turned to walk back to the service station, she wished she didn't feel so annoyingly dejected.

It was Mildred Wilson's telling her of the Chance's importance to the local economy that caused her miserable feelings. She didn't care that Heath Oakes and Dr. Jessica Henderson were preparing for a romantic getaway. She returned to the service station, paid the attendant for the gas and oil, and headed the old Jeep back to the Chance.

****

At six o'clock she heard a vehicle approaching. She glanced out the kitchen window, saw the Cherokee coming into the yard, and returned to the stove for a last check on supper. She'd expected Heath to go to his cabin and was surprised when the vehicle stopped at the Lodge's back door.

When he stepped into the kitchen, she turned from placing a tray of biscuits in the oven and stopped, astonished. He was carrying a dozen yellow roses.

"Hello." She thrust her hands into the pockets of the apron she was wearing over her jeans. Then, "You're staring."

"You're cooking?" His tone reflected amazement.

"Sure." She leaned back against a counter, crossed her arms, and shrugged. "My mother taught me. She's famous for her dinner parties."

"Do you think it might stretch to fill two plates? I haven't eaten since breakfast."

"Really?" She turned to check on a casserole in the oven. "I thought you might have had a lunch date with Dr. Henderson."

"Jesse? Oh, we grabbed a bowl of oyster stew at O'Brien's Cafe." He advanced across the room. When

Allison turned from checking the beef Burgundy warming in the oven with the biscuits, she found him almost touching her. "What would give you that idea?" Curiosity and suspicion colored his inquiry.

"Dr. Henderson's mother remarked about your having a relationship when I went to the clinic looking for you." *Don't look at me like that, as if you can see right through me, right through my ridiculous thoughts.* "Dinner's almost ready. And there is enough for two."

"Thank you. By the way, these are for you." He moved the roses into her arms.

"Really?" A rush of sexual anticipation overwhelmed her before suspicion took its place. *What are you up to?*

"They're a peace offering. I've done some thinking and realized Jack would be miserable if he knew we were squabbling over all he held dear. Let's leave it to the lawyers to hash out."

It didn't seem possible. Heath Oakes was behaving like a gentleman, even apologizing...sort of.

"We do need to talk...rationally," she said.

"I agree. But not until after dinner. Whatever it is, it smells much too fine to be overshadowed by a business discussion." He flashed her a smile designed to melt the hardest heart, then turned toward the door. "Give me ten minutes," he called back over his shoulder. "I want to shower. Oh, by the way, those roses? They're fresh." He let the door slam shut behind him.

His words reviving the memory of the secondhand flowers he'd salvaged for a nasty rich girl years earlier, Allison watched from the kitchen as he strode across to his cottage in the early evening twilight. After the lights

118

had flashed on, through the unshaded windows of both kitchens she saw him pull off his jacket, then his shirt, and pause, bare-chested, to get a glass of water at the sink.

Wow! I bet her royal rottenness wouldn't scoff at him now. She looked down at the dozen golden blooms in her arms. *Flowers. A shower before dinner. He's definitely up to something. Tread carefully, Allison Armstrong. Tread very carefully.* She steeled herself as she reached into a cupboard for a vase. *Whatever it is, it's not going to work.*

She had placed the casserole and biscuits on the table and was returning to the kitchen to set up the coffeepot when he returned. She pushed through the swinging door as he stepped through the outer one. And caught her breath.

Instead of his usual bush pants he was wearing jeans—jeans that would have sold a million copies had he been the model for the brand—and a faded blue chambray shirt soft enough to emphasize every line of his broad shoulders and powerful chest. A hand-tooled brown leather belt at his narrow waist was inlaid with wildlife motifs. His hair, fresh from that shower he'd mentioned, had been brushed and looked so soft Allison felt a sudden, startling desire to run her fingers through its waves and curls.

"Dinner's ready." *Damn.* Her voice sounded surprised, squeaky.

"Good. I've brought wine." He held up a decanter. "I opened it so it can breathe. It's Jack's homemade elderberry."

****

"This is great," he said half way through his second

plate. "You're full of surprises, Allison Armstrong. I never would have suspected you were a gourmet chef. More wine?"

"Please." She extended her glass. Already it was helping to wash away her guilt about her lack of visits to her grandfather, her image of Heath with the beautiful Jessica Henderson, and even her worries about the village's economic future. "For being a homemade variety, it's really very good. And unique."

"Jack used to start with four quarts of crushed elderberries, then add four pounds of sugar and a couple of oranges and lemons. Next he'd dissolve some yeast in water and pour it over a slice of toast. He'd let this float on top of the mixture for about four days and stir it every twenty-four hours. Then he'd strain and bottle it. Four weeks later it was ready. A lot of our guests request it."

"Interesting," she said and took another sip. "Are elderberries as good as their wine?"

"They have a pleasant enough taste," he said. "But they'll never surpass blueberries or wild strawberries. The wine is the best part of them. I'll show you where they grow…if you'll run the river with me."

He looked over at her, golden-brown gaze issuing a subtle challenge.

"Run the North Passage in May?" She put her glass down with a bump. "No way. Aside from the fact that it's too dangerous, I don't have the time. I have to get back to Toronto tomorrow."

"Remember the other time I dared you to do it?"

"And Gramps stopped us before you could taunt me into making one very big mistake."

"I could have gotten us through." He leaned back

in his chair.

"Right. A sixteen-year-old city kid with more machismo than brains," she scoffed.

"I was strong for my age, and Jack had taught me well."

"Maybe, but I'm glad he caught us before we could shove off. I don't think I'd ever seen Gramps so angry."

"Yeah." Heath shifted his shoulders and grinned. "He gave me one hell of a carding out after you left. Told me any part of me that touched you would be in danger of amputation."

"Gramps said that?" Allison felt heat flooding up her face. She'd never suspected her gentle Gramps could talk that way.

"Sure did." A grin curled one corner of his mouth. "And I had no reason to doubt it. Your grandfather might have been a gentle giant around you, but among men he was one tough customer."

"Anyhow, Gramps was right, then, and I know it now, so no way." *Why isn't there some way the human body can control a humiliating blush?*

"O...kay." He drawled out the word, the grin turning to a smirk.

"Hey, look, I'm not afraid. Never mind that it would be madness, I have a previous obligation, that's all."

"Fine." But again his voice held the same annoying inflection.

With an exasperated sigh, she picked up her glass and drained it. Grabbing the decanter she treated herself to a refill.

By the time they'd finished eating, he'd managed to soothe her annoyance, and they were talking about the expected guests and necessary preparations.

"Never mind coffee," he said, standing. "I'll take the wine into the living room and light a fire."

"Fine." She arose. "I'll put these plates in the kitchen before I join you."

Humming, Allison carried the dishes and cutlery out of the dining room. She found her hips swaying to her tune as she put them into the dishwasher. What a lovely evening this was turning out to be! When she returned to the dining room for the empty casserole, biscuit basket, and butter plate, an urge to dance tickled her feet, but she decided that waltzing into the living room might not be the thing to do.

She found him leaning against the mantel, a fire crackling on the hearth, their filled wine glasses on the coffee table in front of it. Soft music wafted from a battery-powered CD player on a table near the garden doors.

Darkness had fallen. A huge globe of a moon rose above the river and trees. Its rays fell over the lawn and through the windows to be swallowed up in the dancing play of light and shadow cast from the hearth.

Tell me this isn't romantic. And he looks so... Feeling lightheaded, Allison sat down abruptly on the couch. She looked up at Heath and remembered how very much she had loved him...once...before...

Struggling to set the thought aside, she picked up her wine and took a long drink. It was as delicious as the first glass.

"I called Myra while I was in town today," he said. "I wanted to let her know you were safe."

"That was thoughtful." *He's got to be the earthiest, most deliciously sexy creature alive.*

An image crossed her mind, an image of a too-thin teenager in a shabby suit, a bouquet of wilted flowers clutched in hand, his expression mirroring the excruciating pain of having his hopes and expectations destroyed in a single moment of abject cruelty.

Heartless wench! She fought a hint of tears threatening her eyes. Dwelling on the past wouldn't help, and she couldn't erase it. But she could work on fixing up the present.

"Want to dance, cowboy?"

"What?"

"I said, Want to dance?"

"Sure, why not?" He stood in front of her.

She polished off what was left in her glass, got to her feet, weaving, and found herself in his arms.

For a moment he gazed down at her, remarkable eyes staring deep into hers, then slowly and sensuously he began to move to the rhythm of the music, easing her into sync with his movements, drawing her full length against him. Aware of every frontal inch of his amazing body, Allison melted, dissolved into the wonderful sensations he was creating. She barely noticed when he danced them out onto the verandah, the full moon over his shoulder mesmerizing her along with the man in her arms.

His lips found her temple, her earlobe. She gasped as his hands slipped from her waist to her hips to thrust them into his.

"You're a good dancer," she said, pulling out from him with a monumental force of will, out from his mind-swirling, solar-plexus-crazing being.

"When I went to university, Jack saw to it that I had decent clothes and enough money to buy fresh flowers." His voice sounded soft as a cat's purr. "As a result, I found a few ladies who were willing to teach me."

"I just bet you did."

She looked up to see the intensity of his attention focused on her. She turned to putty: soft, warm, malleable putty she wanted him to mold. As he drew her back against him in time to the music, it was easy to let sexual instincts take control. Paul never looked at her like that, not when they were dancing, not ever.

"You smell...wonderful," she murmured and missed a step. "Fresh and clean...not like a bottle of three-hundred-dollar cologne."

"And that's a good thing?" His lips brushed her hair.

"I hate that over-priced junk."

She was having an all-out battle with her words, but she didn't care. With his body and his lips and his eyes making her head swirl until her legs no longer wanted to hold her up, speech wasn't a major concern.

"Heath Oakes, I think you're trying to she-...seduce me."

"How am I doing? Are you sufficiently under my spell to reconsider running the river with me?" His words and eyes changed in an instant, had become deadly serious.

"No way! Bugs and bushes and no bathrooms? Forget that idea, cowboy. After a couple of days in the woods, a body gets so dirty and smelly there's no possib...prob...there's no way a person could get romantic. And, right now, I'm feeling very romantic. What about you? Is it true what they say about o...oysters?"

124

Chapter Eight

Allison awoke to the feeling that she had eaten a huge chunk of cotton wool and most of it was still clinging to her tongue and the roof of her mouth. A dehydrating sun blazed down, filtered from her face by a circular fabric dome.

She tried to raise her arms but found she was swaddled in something soft that would have been too warm if it had not been for a coolness at her back. And she was moving, gliding backward, to the sound of moving water.

What happened? Where am I? Frantic, she wrenched against her restraints. The Tilly hat that had served as a blind fell from her face.

"Easy. You'll upset us." His voice stopped her struggles.

Hands gripped her shroud, pulling her to a sitting position. Half blinded by a mid-morning sun, she faced a dark silhouette topped with a Snowy River hat. As her vision returned, she recognized him. She was in a canoe caught in the current of a fast-flowing river with the last man on earth she wanted to be anywhere with. A wilderness of forest covered both banks.

"Oh, my God! What have you done? Where are we?" she rasped out the words, then coughed and grimaced. Her throat felt like sandpaper. Her head drummed a pounding ache.

"Headed down the North Passage," he said. "Here." He reached under his seat and pulled out a canteen. "You need a drink...of water."

He unscrewed the cap as she managed to free her arms from the sleeping bag. When he extended the container toward her, she snatched it from his hand. Throwing back her head, she gobbled. The ice cold water was the best she'd ever tasted.

"Easy," he said. "You'll make yourself sick."

When she ignored his advice, he wrenched it out of her hands.

"Give it back!" She lunged at him. Hobbled by the sleeping bag, she stumbled headlong into him. The canoe rolled, sides all but dipping below water level with each lurch.

"Do something!" Allison grabbed the gunwales. "We're going to upset!"

"Sit quiet." He shoved her back into sitting position, grabbed his paddle, and, with a few deft strokes, stabilized the craft.

"What have you done?" When they were once more moving smoothly down the river, she stared at the water and wilderness that surrounded them.

"I've shanghaied you." He put aside his paddle, picked up the canteen, and took a swallow before recapping it.

"Kidnapped, you mean." Outrage surmounted all her previous emotions.

"No, shanghaied." He plunged his paddle deep, sending the canoe to the right to avoid a rock. "You'll be working your passage."

"Oh, I don't think so. And for future reference, what did you do while I was out cold?" she raged.

"Loaded you into a sleeping bag and this canoe." He kept his eyes focused over her head, at the river beyond. "Check your clothes if you're concerned. I've never been turned on by an inebriated woman."

"I was not inebriated, you backstreet slim. Ouch!" Her outburst brought on a pounding ache above her eyes. She caught her head between her hands. "Take me back to the Lodge right now! Otherwise, I'll have you charged with kidnapping!"

"Really? I'm shaking in my boots. You'll feel better after you've had a couple of aspirin and some lunch."

"Don't you dare laugh at me!" She clenched her fists and sucked in her lips. "I'm deadly serious!"

"Well, then, that's too bad. Because I can't take you back. We're a good six miles downriver from the Lodge, deep into roadless wilderness, and with the force of the freshet that's pushing us, a superhero couldn't paddle us back upstream." He dipped his paddle deep and nosed the canoe to the left.

"Hang on," he ordered. "We're heading into rapids."

Allison glanced over her shoulder just in time to be hit full in the face with the spray from the first wave of white froth. She gasped and swung back on Heath, water running down her cheeks, ready to yell more incriminations. His expression stopped her. Mind and body, he was concentrated on controlling their craft over the turbulence.

Through the next few minutes that seemed like a lifetime, the canoe bucked over rapids and skittered around protruding rocks like a thing possessed. All she could do was cling to the sides and give thanks she was seated backwards and couldn't see what was coming next. The only comfort she could find was in remembering Heath was a veteran canoeist—one of the best, her grandfather had told her.

When they finally reached the calmer waters of a pool on the far side, she slumped against the back of the canoe's front bench.

"I thought...I thought we were going to capsize," she choked, feeling overwhelmed by the situation. Suddenly her stomach revolted. She leaned over the side and retched. *Oh, God, is it possible to feel more miserable?*

"We're okay, and we'll be okay." His voice was calm, reassuring. "You got a little wet, that's all. It was my fault. We wouldn't have hit that white water at the angle we did if I'd been paying attention. We'll go to shore, you can freshen up, and I'll make lunch. Strong coffee, a couple of aspirin, a sandwich, and fresh clothes will make that hangover a lot better."

"Where's Jack?" The thought hit her as she wiped her mouth with the back of her hand. "What have you done with Jack?"

"He's a great dog, but hardly a wilderness type. I put him in the care of the couple of guys I've left manning Chance Lodge. His dog-sitters are both dyed-in-the-wool canine fanciers. He'll be fine."

He swung the prow of the canoe shoreward. In a few minutes, Allison was standing on the riverbank and realizing for the first time she still wore the jeans, sweatshirt, and sneakers she'd put on twenty-four hours earlier. Only now they were wet and rumpled, and she felt sweaty and dirty and all out grungy.

She watched as Heath pulled the canoe well above

the waterline, noted the knife in a scabbard at his belt, and shivered. While she might pity him as the underprivileged teenager he'd once been, she realized he was also the adult version of a child so consumed with rage against the affluent he'd led police on a life-and-death car chase.

"Here." He threw her a waterproof packsack. "There's a spring about fifty yards back in the trees, over to the left. You can wash up and change. You'll find everything you need in the bag. Jesse got it ready."

"It seems Dr. Henderson did a great deal toward arranging this voyage of the damned," she muttered, reaching for the pack and feeling her head pound as she straightened up. "I bet she signed Gramps' death certificate, too, and recommended no autopsy."

"She did." Heath turned from his task and looked at her, squinting in the sunlight. "Under New Brunswick law, none is required in cases like Jack's, where he'd been under a physician's care for a serious illness that obviously was the cause of death, unless the family requests one and pays for it. Your father and mother didn't see any need for one under those circumstances. By the way, you'll find aspirin in there for that hangover."

"Hangover! I'm not hung over! I'm…"

"Go."

She could only attempt to glare at him, hampered by the sun behind him glinting on the sparkling water and making her eyes hurt and her head ache even harder. With a disgruntled mutter, she turned and headed off in the direction he'd indicated for the spring.

When she reached the place where crystal-clean water bubbled out of a hillside, she knelt and splashed handfuls over her hot face. *Blessed relief.* Then she turned and opened the valise. Inside she was amazed to find toiletries and spanking new clothing appropriate to wilderness travel.

Several white T-shirts, three plaid flannel shirts, three pair of bush pants, a leather belt, a down-filled vest, a weatherproof jacket with a hood, both cotton and woolen socks, a pair of hiking boots, a package of feminine hygiene products, and even some highly practical underwear had been carefully packed into the sack. Mildred Wilson had racked up an excellent sale yesterday.

Digging deep, she discovered shampoo, toothpaste and toothbrush, soap, a brush and comb, and even deodorant nestled in a plastic bag wrapped in a towel and face cloth.

First needs first. She uncapped the aspirin, popped a couple into her mouth, then cupped her hands, filled them with spring water, and washed the pills down her throat.

Lord, I feel grungy. She glanced about at the spring's surroundings. Secluded by a circle of close-growing alders, it offered privacy of a sort. Although she loathed him, she knew Heath Oakes was no sexual predator. Hadn't he had a perfect opportunity when she'd—she shuddered to admit it—passed out from too much of that potent wine? And being a peeping Tom definitely wasn't his style.

She pulled off her sweaty, rumpled clothes. Bathing every inch of her aching, weary body in fresh, pure, albeit icy water would revive her. Naked, she began to wash.

Twenty minutes later she was feeling much better.

As she pulled the vest over the plaid shirt, with the white T-shirt peeping out at its throat, she couldn't help grinning. In this getup even Myra wouldn't recognize her. She brushed her teeth, ran a comb through her damp hair, and hefted her packsack, ready to return to their campsite.

A twig snapped in the bush to her left.

She whirled but saw only a thicket budding into leaf. Nothing stirred. But no birds sang, either. Jack had taught her that kind of silence in the bush wasn't good.

An eerie feeling wafted over her. She felt the hair on the back of her neck prickle. Was it a bear? A ravenous, fresh-out-of-hibernation bear looking for food, any kind of food? Or was it maybe that weird being she and Marty Mason had glimpsed on their way to the Chance?

Bear. It had to be a bear. There were no such creatures as sasquatches. Remembering her grandfather's first rule of bear defense, she eased off her Tilly hat and whirled it toward the spot from which the sound had issued. Then she turned and raced back to where she'd left Heath.

She ran full tilt into him as he arose from lighting the camp stove. With a grunt, he caught her in his arms.

"What happened?" he asked. When she could only gasp and point back into the bush, he shook her. "What happened?"

"Bear!" she gasped.

"Did you see it?" His hand went to the knife at his belt.

"No…no. I heard it…in the bush."

"Oh." He released her and turned back to the stove.

"Oh, right!" She began to get her breath back

131

enough to be angry. "Silly city girl wouldn't know a bear if she fell over it."

"If it were a bear, you wouldn't have heard it." He adjusted the gas as a flame leaped up. "I've seen a four-hundred-pounder move as silently as a shadow."

"But no birds were singing!"

"What?" He snapped around to face her.

"No birds were singing. Gramps always said that meant a predator was near."

"I'm glad you remember one of Jack's lessons. What did you do after you decided it was a bear? Run?"

"Of course not. Not until I threw my hat in his direction to give him something to sniff and me a head start."

"You *did* listen to Jack." Satisfaction brightened his tone.

"Yes, yes, yes!" Exasperation overpowered fear. "Aren't you going to investigate? Aren't you going to…"

"Take on a bear with a knife, a hatchet, and a can of pepper spray? They're the only weapons I have. I'm not that heroic. I'll go back and get your hat after we eat. You'll be needing it. By that time, whatever you heard will be gone."

"Ahhhhh!" She plunked herself down on the shore and clasped her hands on top of her head. He was the most frustrating creature she'd ever met. And that included several green-broke horses.

"Those clothes fit pretty good." He glanced over at her as he put coffee on to brew. "For only having met you once, Jess did a great job of sizing you up. You smell nice, too. Guess she has good taste in whatever that stuff is."

"You arranged all this yesterday when you went to town, didn't you? The roses were only a ploy to soften me up, to get me to trust you, and drink that Harvey Wallbanger of a wine."

"Elderberry." A smirk curled one corner of his mouth. "If you had been familiar with wine made from local berries, you might have taken it a little easier."

"Oh, and that fact lessens your culpability?" She rested her back against a log and stretched her legs out in front of her.

"No." He took a couple of sandwiches out of a plastic container, put them into a frying pan, and set it on the stove's second burner. "But it does explain why I had only a couple of glasses and managed to stay awake. Careful, that's hot." He stopped her as she reached for the coffeepot.

"I'm so thirsty and hungry I could swallow molten lava," she said but drew back and waited for him to serve her the coffee in a tin mug, along with the toasted ham-and-cheese sandwich on a plastic plate. She took a sip of the steaming brew, bit into the sandwich, then closed her eyes and munched in ecstasy.

"Mmmmmm," she moaned with pleasure. "Food from the gods couldn't taste any better."

"I wouldn't go that far." He joined her against the log, his own coffee and sandwich in hand. "But there is a special something about food cooked and eaten in the outdoors. Especially after a fifteen-hour fast."

"Fifteen hours? What time it is? How long did I sleep?"

"It's shortly after noon. You only slept a few hours, Rip Van Winkle. Don't worry. You haven't aged perceptibly."

"Clever, aren't you?" She paused in wolfing down her lunch and glared at him. "As soon as I've finished eating, I plan to start walking back to the Lodge. All I have to do is follow the river."'

"And cross two ravines with freshet-flooded streams and temperatures so cold they will kill anyone foolish enough to try to cross them at this time of year." He replenished his cup and hers. "Hypothermia isn't a pleasant way to go."

"So I'm trapped here...with you?"

"Looks like it." He sipped his coffee, watching her over the rim of his mug.

"Well, don't expect any romantic moments, buddy!" She stacked her cup and plate beside him and leaned back against the log. "Not if you were the last man on earth and the human race were about to become extinct."

"Fine by me." He gathered her dishes with his and stood. "All I want you to do is enjoy the ride, drink in the ambience, and allow yourself to develop an appreciation for the surroundings. You can get started while I pack up our gear."

Allison drew a deep breath of clear, cool spring air lightly flavored with the scents of burgeoning greenery. Just this once it wouldn't hurt to do as he instructed.

Maples and birches, their buds already beginning to fan out with the promise of new leaves, surrounded their landing site. Riverside ferns and grasses, too, were becoming verdant with rebirth. Even the alders along the riverbank in places still flooded with the freshet showed promise of renewed life. Swinging with cavalier devil-may-care joy from a nearby branch white-furred with pussywillows, a red-winged blackbird burst into song.

The May sun warmed her, the utter peace of her surroundings lulled her. High-rise offices, pressure-cooker meetings, heels, tailored business suits, spa and hair appointments, and incessantly ringing phones slid from her mind. She relaxed and dozed.

****

She jerked awake to see Heath had unpacked the canoe and set up a tent. A fire crackled inside a circle of rocks near the river's edge. As she scrambled to her feet, he straightened from adding a log to it.

In the twilight, silhouetted against the primitive force of the river's wild rush, he was an imposing figure, tall, muscular, and lithe, a true man of the wilderness. He made her pulses speed, her solar plexus tighten.

"We're staying here?" She suppressed a shiver. The sun had disappeared behind the trees across the river, leaving a distinct chill in the air.

"It's as good a place as any we'll find for a few miles," he said. "And since you slept most of the day away…"

"You could have awakened me!" she snapped, rubbing her arms. "Now it will take us even longer to get to the end of this miserable voyage."

"The longer I keep you out here, the better the chances you'll start to appreciate all this. You're cold and cranky. Come over by the fire. It will help the first part."

"I am not crank…" Allison caught herself. *How childish can I sound?*

"Fine. Stay where you are." He hunkered down beside the fire and stirred it to new heights with a stick.

135

She hesitated, shivered again, then, feeling a strange moth-to-the-flame apprehension, moved to join him.

"It's peaceful here." She sat down beside him. "Even with the river at full flood."

"Glad you noticed." He quirked her a grin, and this time it wasn't sardonic.

"It's been years since I've seen a bonfire." With a sigh, she rested her chin on arms braced against her bent knees as she gazed into the flames. Serenity slid over her.

"Damn it!" She snapped out of it and rounded on him. "Did you slip something into my coffee at noon?"

"If you have to attribute your pleasure in the moment to drugs, I'm wasting my time."

He stood and strode toward the trees into the deepening shadows. When he vanished from sight, Allison felt a surge of panic. *Where is he going? What if he never comes back? What if he's leaving me to die in the wilderness? Have I insulted him once too often? Oh, God, what have I done?*

Breathe, breathe. If he'd been planning to leave me, he could have done it while I was asleep. She glanced at the dark outline of the canoe and realized leaving her wasn't in his plans. He wouldn't desert her without taking the canoe.

What was that? She swung toward the place where he'd vanished into the forest.

He emerged out of the shadows, a package of wieners, a bag of rolls, a tube of mustard, a sack of marshmallows, and two bottles of lime soda in his arms.

"I put our coolers up in the trees a few yards

away." He squatted by the fire and spread out the food. "They've got tight covers and shouldn't attract bears. Still, there's no point in inviting them up to our tent."

"Lime?" She gazed at the bottles of her favorite soda.

"You loved the stuff. I couldn't understand why. After you left, I'd drink a bottle every once in a while to see what there was to like about it. Eventually, I acquired a taste."

"Really?" *The man was nothing if not full of surprises.*

"Yeah, really." There was no warmth in his tone. When he pulled the knife from its scabbard at his belt, she gasped.

"Look, what I said earlier about your drugging my lunch…" She fell back, away from him.

"Take it easy." He checked its blade against his finger. "I'm going to cut a couple of dogwood branches to use as roasting sticks. Hell, you really do have a sick opinion of me."

"You did get me drunk, you did kidnap me…"

"Shanghaied. There's a difference, remember. You'll be free to do whatever you wish at the end of the voyage, no ransom required."

"Whatever. Furthermore, you're the last person to see my grandfather alive, you've profited handsomely from his death, and you'd be only too happy to get rid of a business partner who doesn't share your future plans for that inheritance. My mother will be furious when she finds out what you've done!"

"She knows." Satisfied with the knife's sharpness, he returned it to its sheath.

"Mom knows…that you filled me full of wine, that

137

you're taking me on this voyage of the damned against my will?" Allison was appalled.

"She knows we're running the river." He faced her squarely. "I told her what I planned to do when I spoke to her on the telephone yesterday. She thought it was a good idea to jog your memory of all your grandfather held dear. She also thought I'd be able to convince you verbally to come along. When that failed, I had to resort to other methods. She doesn't know about that last part."

"Do you think she'll condone what you actually did? Do you honestly think—"

"No," he said. "If you were my daughter, I'd be ready to beat the living daylights out of any man who 'spirited' away my child. But you're not my child, and I'm confident the end will justify the means."

He turned and once more strode off into the darkness. Allison sank back down on the riverbank gravel. This entire mess read like something out of a cliché adventure novel. Heroine captured by handsome savage and carried away into the wilderness to become his adoring mate.

She drew her knees up in front of her, folded her arms on top of them once again, and watched the flames diminishing into coals—red-hot, glowing coals perfect for roasting wieners and marshmallows. She remembered her last meal cooked over a bonfire.

Gramps had been there. And her mother and Heath and his mother. It had been the second to last night she'd spent at the Chance, and after they'd eaten she and Heath had wandered down by the boathouse, a full summer moon lighting their way. She'd been fourteen, that age when boys are an endless fascination, and

Heath, at sixteen, had seemed very much a man of the world, a romantic rebel full of inner-city toughness and street savvy.

She recalled leaning back against the rounded logs of the boathouse, the moonlight on her face, her waist-length wavy hair falling in cascades over her shoulders. Heath had come to stand close in front of her, a dark silhouette between the wild river and the romantic light of the moon. Feet planted apart, he'd towered above her, his shadow enveloping her, the planes of his face strong and handsome in the shadows.

The soft summer night filled with silvery magic. From the riverbanks, frogs raised a chorus to the young lovers. A tender breeze rippled sensuous music through the pines. And when Heath took her into his arms and touched his lips to hers, all her naive fantasies burst into full bloom. She remembered the way her heartbeat had gone into a wild flurry, the butterflies that had danced in her stomach, and, below, an overwhelming feeling of ecstasy she'd never before experienced. It had whirled her out of reality.

Heath was in love with her! Wild joy burst over her in an enchanted wave. Nothing could have been more wonderful, more perfect.

But suddenly his embrace tightened. She was pinned against the boathouse by his taut body. His mouth came down on hers again, but this time it was hard and brutal. He forced her lips apart, his tongue into her mouth. One hand went under her T-shirt, sliding up her back, working at her bra clasp. His body forced against hers was hard, shocking, demanding more than she could have imagined.

"What are you doing? Let me go!" She struggled,

but somehow he pinned her hands behind her back with one of his.

"Come on, baby. I know the signs. You've been inviting this all night." His arms became steel bands, his chest a brick wall. He bent his head to kiss her again, but this time she was ready. She clamped her teeth down on his lower lip.

He howled and staggered back from her.

"Bitch!" he snarled, scrubbing at the blood seeping down his chin. "Snotty rich bitch! Get away from me. Go on, run back to your fancy house and clothes!"

For a moment she stood staring at him. He was no longer handsome, no longer exciting and romantic. His features, in the shifting shadows, took on the threatening sneer of a wolf. He was a beast—a horrible, nasty beast.

With a stifled sob, she turned and ran toward the Lodge, stumbling over roots, tears streaming down her face. She was relieved to find her family and Mrs. Oakes hadn't yet returned. Rushing to her room, she slammed the door, locked it, and fell face down onto her bed.

"I'll never, ever feel romantic about any man as long as I live," she sobbed into her pillow. "Falling in love is just something stupid people write about in books, stupid, stupid books!"

She'd never told anyone what had happened. She'd been too ashamed.

****

The howl of a coyote startled her back to the present, and Allison glanced over her shoulder into the darkness. A form emerged, a form that was Heath.

"Here." He handed her a pointed stick. "The coals

140

look ready."

"Sure…okay." She took the slender branch and reached for the package of wieners.

Her fingers fumbled with the plastic packaging, and suddenly he was squatting in front of her, covering her trembling hands with his.

"Allie, what's wrong?"

In the glow of the dying fire she couldn't see his face distinctly, but his use of her grandfather's pet name softened her to the heart.

"Nothing… A coyote howled."

"Level with me…for once." His tone brooked no denial.

"I was…remembering." She let the package drop from her hands and allowed her gaze to rest on his hands clasped over hers. "Our last wiener roast."

"Allie…" The word came in a soft, aching breath. "God, Allie, I'm sorry."

"W…what?"

"For what I did that night. I was fresh out of a tough juvenile facility where forcing yourself on a girl was considered the macho thing to do, and, after Jennifer, I was out to take my revenge on the first rich girl who crossed my path."

Allison felt his fingers beneath her chin. When he raised her face to a level with his, she hated the tears she felt brimming in her eyes.

"You…you destroyed my spirit of romance," she choked. "You took away all the mystery and magic. You were the reason I never came back to the Chance. I couldn't stand the sight of you!"

"You're telling me I'm the reason you never came back to visit Jack? Sweet Jesus, Allie!" His eyes stared deep into hers, so deep he might be looking down into her soul.

"It doesn't matter now. There's no going back. I can't undo the loneliness Gramps suffered. I can't get that magic back in my heart." Those damn tears slid down her cheeks.

"Don't." He leaned forward to touch his lips to hers. "Please, Allie, don't. I can't watch you hurt any more."

Astonished by his tenderness for a moment, she didn't speak. Then she shrugged away, wiped the tears with the back of her hand, and looked down at the package of wieners on the gravel between them.

"Just forget it, okay? Open the wieners. I assume your knife is still sharp?" She sniffed herself back into control.

"Right." He picked up the celluloid pack in one hand, pulled his knife from its scabbard with the other, and, in a single, swift gesture, slit it open. "Here." He handed it back to her. "Eat."

Their second pair of wieners were browning over the coals before he spoke again.

"Dogwood," he said.

"What?" Surprised, she looked over at him as he squatted across the fire pit from her.

"These sticks we're using, they're dogwood, probably the hardest wood of all time. Their branches were once used to make daggers and were known as dagger wood. Time corrupted it to dogwood."

"Interesting," she replied vaguely, returning her gaze to the roasting wiener.

"Another legend states it was named dogwood because it proved effective in curing mange in dogs."

"Charming." She glanced over at him and, even in the flickering light, caught the gleam of mischief in his eyes.

He removed the cooked wiener from its skewer, plunked in into a roll, and applied mustard. Then he picked up the half-empty bottle of lime soda beside him and took a drink. "Hard to believe I like this stuff."

"Given time, I suppose a person can develop a taste for almost anything." She bit into her hot dog. "I'd forgotten how good these can be."

"Nothing like food cooked in the outdoors. There's a lot more you'll discover you've been missing, if you'll give yourself a chance to experience it."

"I said I'd forgotten how good these can be. I didn't say I'd never had better or that I wanted a steady diet of them."

"Okay." He finished his hot dog and handed her a cellophane bag. "Here, roast a marshmallow. Might sweeten your disposition."

He stood ten minutes later. "Don't forget to bury the tip of your stick in the sand. Bears can smell sweet stuff a long way off."

He skewered his own cooking stick into the earth, stretched, yawned, picked up a cooking pot, and headed for the river. Shortly he returned and doused the campfire with its contents. As a cloud of smoke gusted up into the cold, crisp air, he dropped the container and offered a hand to help her to her feet.

"Time to hit the tent."

"You do that. I'll be in when I'm ready." She ignored his gesture.

"Suit yourself." He shrugged and turned toward the tent. "But it'll get cold and scary out here without a fire to keep the frost and bears at bay."

For a few minutes after he'd vanished into the tent, Allison sat stubbornly on the shore. A thin trickle of smoke wafted wreath-like from the smothering embers. Cold night air wrapped about her. In spite of her down-filled vest and flannel shirt, she shivered.

I won't go rushing to join him. I won't let him think I'm cold or afraid.

An owl hooted. A coyote raised a cry in the blackness beyond their campsite. Its long, mournful howl invited others to join a chorus. Allison stumbled to her feet, glancing back into the dark trees.

Maybe I should go to bed.

A slight movement to her left caught her attention. She turned toward the river. In the moonlight, something huge and hairy stood slouched and ape-like in the shallows.

A rock-like lump of terror blocked her voice. Rooted in place, she stared.

The creature shuffled toward her, then paused, appeared to sniff the air, and grunted.

A sasquatch. It's definitely a sasquatch!

She bent and grabbed the end of a stick protruding from the smoldering fire. In the darkness its tip glowed red.

"Get!" She thrust it toward the creature.

"Allison, come on. Enough sulking. It's got to be cold out there."

Heath's voice from the tent stopped the creature. It grunted again, shook a paw in her direction, then turned and waddled off into the darkness downriver.

As it disappeared, Allison dropped the stick back into the fire pit. Turning, she scrambled toward the tent.

"Sasquatch!" she cried as she fumbled with its zippered door.

"What?" Heath bolted upright in his sleeping bag when she burst inside.

"Sasquatch! In the river!"

"Stay here." He came to his feet, his hand on the knife at his belt, and ducked out of the tent.

She sank down on the bed he'd laid out across from his, drew up knees too weak to support her, and hugged herself into a ball. Shivering, she rocked to and fro.

"Nothing out there." A dark silhouette against the brighter outdoors, he stooped back into the tent. "I'll look for tracks in the morning." He zipped the canvas door flap shut.

"There won't be any. He...it was standing in the shallows."

"Right." Exasperation colored the word. "I should have guessed. Did it dive out of sight...like the Loch Ness Monster?"

"You don't believe me!"

"You make it difficult. First, a noisy bear. Now an amphibious sasquatch. Do me a favor. Get some sleep. And don't wake me when you hear a poltergeist." With a grunt, he climbed into his bed.

Muttering expletives, Allison pulled off her boots and crawled into her own sleeping bag. The bubble mattress crackled in tune with her temper.

Chapter Nine

Allison awoke to bird song and the gurgle of river water. Sunlight filtered through the tent to fall in a warming bath over her face. Freeing her arms from her sleeping bag, she stretched them above her head and drew a deep breath of crisp, clear air, a sense of contentment engulfing her.

She pulled herself up onto one elbow to look over to where Heath had been lying when she fell asleep. He was gone, his sleeping bag neatly rolled up atop his bubble mattress.

Stretching again, she stood. And shivered. She grabbed her vest that had served as a pillow and pulled it on. Spring in this country still boasted frosty nights that left a distinct nip in the morning air.

Coffee. I need a cup of hot, black coffee.

She unzipped the door flap and stepped out into a dazzling green spring morning where water droplets from melting frost glistened jewel-like on grass and trees. The sky boasted a flawless blue, and the river swept past in wild, majestic abandon. And squatted beside it, Heath Oakes, naked down to the waist, was splashing its icy water over his face and upper body. When he stood to towel himself dry, silhouetted against the surging water, he brought the words "noble savage" racing across her mind.

Get a grip. Remember what he did when you were

a romantic teenager. Remember the hurt he caused Jack because of it. Remember what a mess you're in right now because of him.

Running a hand through her tangled hair, she started toward him.

A noble savage wouldn't have shanghaied me. A noble savage wouldn't have scoffed at my fears last night.

"Good morning." He turned at her approach and smiled a flash of perfect white teeth.

"Chilly for river bathing half naked, isn't it?" She had to struggle to keep her gaze off his incredible body.

"I had to." He headed across the gravel to where his packsack lay open. He took from it a snowy white T-shirt and pulled it over his head. "I couldn't risk having you call me filthy or stinking again." His eyes flashed with bitter humor. "A filthy, stinking, street tramp, to be exact."

"I never did!" she gasped as he pulled a flannel shirt from his pack and thrust his arms into it.

"You most certainly did." He buttoned it, narrowing those amazing golden-brown eyes as he looked over at her.

Oh, my God, I remember. I did.

"And what did you call me?" she countered, shame burning up her face in a hot blush. "'Snotty rich brat' isn't exactly complimentary, either!"

"No, but at the time, it was accurate."

"Oh, for God's sake, it was ages ago. Let's just drop it. We both said a lot of things."

"Okay, fine." He looked down at her and something inside did flip-flops at his nearness, his blatant maleness, his intensity. "What happened to your

147

hair?" He reached out to touch the curls hanging below her ears.

She felt her breath catch in her throat. *Don't,* a small warning voice whispered. *Don't let him charm you...again.*

"I cut it."

"It was the stuff romance is made of." His perception startled her, the softness in his tone weakened her defenses. "So you had to get rid of it."

How can he know me so well? Those penetrating eyes seem to be able to see right through to my soul.

He released the curl and stepped away. He tucked his shirttail into his bush pants, pulled on his vest, and headed to where a pot sat steaming on the camp stove.

Damn it, I won't have him getting into my mind. As for what he's doing to my body...

She grabbed her packsack and strode upriver out of his sight to freshen up.

When she finished her morning ablutions, crouched by the river, she paused and gazed about. Memories flooded back with that wonderful sense of awe she'd always felt and shared with her grandfather on mornings such as this.

The full flush of spring surrounded her. Birches and maples, their buds about to burst into leaf, stood laced in soft, transparent halos of palest green against a dark backdrop of spruce and pine. The moss under her hiking boots formed a natural carpeting, the river's lusty rush voicing nature's special baritone. In the branches of a thicket nearby, a flock of chickadees cavorted, chorusing their joy in the perfection of the season.

An osprey squawked as it slanted past her.

Shielding her eyes against the morning sun, Allison watched it settle on its awkward nest of sticks and twigs high atop a dead tree several hundred yards away.

She remembered Gramps telling her the names of trees and birds and plants and animals, teaching her which mushrooms and berries were edible and convincing her that the snakes and frogs and toads that made their home on the Chance were harmless, valuable in keeping the insect population under control.

He'd taught her about the erosion caused by clear cutting of the forests and its far-reaching side effects, preached against sport hunting, and worried aloud about stresses on the environment caused by careless overuse of wilderness areas for recreational activities.

Finally she gathered up her toiletries and arose. She was letting the ambience get to her, and that was tantamount to falling victim to Heath Oakes' plan.

Before she headed back to the campsite, she glanced once more up at the osprey nest and saw its mate lighting beside it on the rim of the crude nest.

Spring. Mating season in the wilderness. She clamped her packsack to her chest and turned away.

Heath had brewed coffee and made French toast, with butter and maple syrup to top it, for breakfast. Allison polished off her second slice and third cup and hated her admission. *Delicious. It's not bad enough the man looks better than a movie star...he can cook. I hope the way to a woman's heart isn't the same way as to a man's...through the stomach. If it is, I could be in trouble.*

When they'd finished eating, he replenished both their mugs and came to sit beside her on a log near the canoe. The sun had chased most of the chill from the air. Allison basked in its warmth.

"Gramps would have enjoyed this morning," she said.

"Definitely." Heath rested his elbows on his drawn-up knees, his coffee mug in his hands, and gazed out at the river. "And appreciated every minute. What about his granddaughter?" He glanced sideways at her before looking down at the coffee cup in his sun-bronzed hands.

"I never said this isn't a gorgeous area, that I didn't recognize its beauty. I just don't want to spend the rest of my life tending it." She stood, splashed the remainder of her coffee out over the grass, and headed for the river to rinse her mug. "Time to start packing. The sooner we get going, the sooner we get to the take-out point and the sooner I get on my way to Toronto."

A half hour later they headed downstream, Allison in the prow, Heath piloting in the stern. As he guided the canoe around rocks, fallen trees, and other debris, she had to admire his skill. High water and strong currents that would have unnerved even experienced canoeists appeared to have little effect on his confidence in his ability.

She felt safe, an inane state of mind given the facts that the river was savage at this time of year and that she still—if only vaguely—suspected the one person capable of keeping her from injury or death of being involved in her grandfather's passing. She wouldn't have felt safe with Paul.

Where did that thought come from? Being shanghaied must have made me incapable of rational thinking. Paul would never force me into a trip like this. Paul would never...

She dipped her paddle deeper. *I could handle this canoe alone if I had to.* But she knew that was a lie. Her survival depended on the man sitting silently behind her.

She was startled out of her reflection as he touched her shoulder with the tip of a dripping paddle. When she turned to him, he held up a silencing finger, then pointed to the shore.

She looked. And gasped.

A massive black bear stood immobile as stone, staring down into a small pool formed by a semicircle of rocks near the shore. Suddenly, with lightning speed, it flashed a paw through the quiet water and flipped something twisting and gleaming onto the shore. Following immediately, the bear seized its catch. With the glistening Atlantic salmon dangling from its jaws, it lumbered into the bush.

"Wow! He's good!" Allison's delight colored her response.

"Could be as a result of thousands of years of practice…genetically speaking." She glanced back at her companion to see a shadow of a smile brightening the lean planes of his face.

"Right." She turned her back to him and took up her paddle. "I'd almost forgotten you're a genuine degree-toting biologist."

"True, but all the really useful stuff I've ever learned came from Jack."

Allison felt her throat constrict. The wilderness was bringing her closer and closer to her grandfather's memory, making her more and more aware of the enormity of her loss.

He never lets up trying to make me remember,

make me feel the way I used to about this country, about Gramps' hopes and dreams for it. He won't succeed. After all, I'm Allison Armstrong, CFO of a major corporation. I'm one tough nut to crack.

"Put your body into it." His voice cut into her thoughts.

"What?"

"Use your entire upper body, not just your arms." He demonstrated. "Otherwise you'll get sore muscles."

The motion brought a rush of memories. Relaxing, she fell into it as easily as she'd done over a dozen years ago when she and her grandfather were running the river, in tune with the country and its inhabitants.

"Good." He gave the canoe a powerful push with his paddle and sent it across the stretch of flat water near the pool the bear had deserted. "Time for lunch. There's a stretch of tricky water ahead. I don't plan to tackle it on an empty stomach."

****

"Here." He swung a cooler out of the beached canoe. "See what you can rustle up."

"What?" She stared at him.

"Time you started acting like a shanghaied person. That means working your way. This isn't one of your luxury cruises."

"I'm well aware of the fact." She stood with her hands on her hips and faced him. "But I'm not about to become your galley slave."

"Slave? You've yet to lift a finger. It's time you got with the program. I'll show you how to light the camp stove. After that, you and the cooler are on your own."

He removed the small stove from the canoe, carried

it a short distance from the shore, and knelt beside it.

"Well?" He looked back at her. "Come on. I haven't got all day."

"Fine." She pulled herself up proudly and marched to join him. "Show me."

Ten minutes later she had water boiling on one burner, soup heating on the second.

Not bad for a city girl. She stood up to survey her handiwork, then gasped as her gaze fell on a promontory farther upriver. A doe and her white spotted baby stood at the water's edge. The youngster was cavorting along the precipice.

"Heath," she called. "Look. The fawn is too near the cliff. Oh, Lord!"

The baby's hooves slipped, the little animal scrambled to regain its footing, then plunged, crying and pawing desperately, down into the roiling water. The doe leaped and screamed.

Images of Pride and her foal slashed across Allison's mind.

"Heath!" she screamed, running to look down at the thrashing fawn, its head bobbing up, then under the water.

She was pulling off her boots when Heath joined her.

"Don't be crazy!" he yelled above the roar of the rapids. "You can't save it!" He grabbed her hands on her boot laces.

"I have to try! It's only a baby!" She struggled to free herself, but he dragged her back from the precipice. "The baby's going to drown!" she screamed up at him. "Don't you realize? The baby is going to drown!"

He looked down at her, gaze scanning her face.

"Ah, damn!" He ran back to the lip of the cliff, sucked in his breath, and leaped, feet first, into the wild, ice-cold river.

The fawn's head bobbed in and out of sight in the angry water. It was losing its fight for life as Heath struggled toward it, water to his armpits.

Her heart hammering, Allison scrambled down stream looking for a place where the shore was accessible. Horrified, she could only watch as the pair, caught in the river's powerful flow, were swept along beside her. *Oh, God, let me get to a shoreline where I can help them...soon.* Her mind swirled like those crazy eddies that were threatening to consume man and fawn.

"Yes!" she yelled when she reached a low embankment and saw Heath grab the fawn and clamp it under his arm. In a split second her delight turned to horror when Heath, caught in the force of the whirling water, stumbled and fell.

"Heath!" she screamed. "Oh, God, Heath!"

She plunged into the icy water, reaching out for him, until, knee deep, she managed to clutch his shirt front. With her pulling, he stumbled to his feet, the little animal clutched under his arm. He staggered against her as she struggled to get them both to shore.

Once on dry land, he released the fawn and collapsed onto the shore, his chest heaving. The little deer shook itself, dog-like, then stood panting and trembling beside the couple. The doe trotted out of the bush and stopped, rigidly alert, one hoof raised as she stared at the trio.

"Here's your baby," Heath rasped. "Come and get him."

The doe snorted. The fawn shook itself again, then

gamboled on wobbly legs to her side. She paused a few seconds to examine her baby before she turned and bounded into the forest, the fawn close behind her.

"Strip." Allison turned her attention back to Heath. He was quaking. Hypothermia leaped into her mind.

"Now? I haven't had any oysters recently." He slanted her an exhausted grin.

"You've got to get out of those wet clothes," she yelled back over her shoulder as she ran toward the canoe. "I'll get our sleeping bags and make a fire."

Fifteen minutes later, Heath was huddled in both sleeping bags as she threw dry sticks onto a crackling fire near the river. She'd gotten it started while he divested himself of wet clothing. Once she felt assured he was comfortable, she'd pulled off her wet boots and socks. Now two pairs of boots huddled near the flames.

"Here." She handed him a steaming mug of soup from the pot she'd been heating when she noticed the deer.

"What made you want to jump into the river after that fawn?" He cradled the mug in hands bleached with cold and looked up at her.

"I love animals," she replied. "I've always had horses and ponies… My dad was a cowboy when he was young. It's in my blood, I guess."

"Cowboy to big-city surgeon. Big leap. I remember. Jack told me about it a lot of years ago. Your grandfather loved animals, too."

"I know." She measured coffee into the other pot. "He taught me about them and their environment. He said he learned his teaching technique from the mistakes he made with his first student."

"First?"

"My mother." She closed her eyes and leaned forward to inhale the aroma of the brewing coffee. "She's an expert canoeist and outdoors person."

"Myra? Hard to visualize under all the sophistication and style."

"You should see her ride." Allison opened her eyes and swung back to face him.

"Ride? As in horses, boots, and saddles?"

Proud of her mother and her accomplishments, she fell into the story of how Myra, until she was twenty-three and a college graduate, had called the Chance her home, how that summer she'd met and fallen in love with a young doctor who was a guest at the Lodge. They'd married and moved to Ottawa, where Cameron Armstrong had gained a reputation as one of the country's leading neurosurgeons.

She told how her mother had become a leading fundraiser for needy sick children and how, in her spare time, Myra Armstrong had taken up riding to be able to accompany her husband, whose chief form of recreation still reflected his cowboy roots.

The story of her own riding career came out, too. She told him about Pride and, finally, haltingly about the death of little Joy.

"When I saw that doe's distress, it all came back to me in a rush." She feigned attention on the coffeepot. "I couldn't allow another animal to suffer like Pride." She drew a deep breath and hefted her shoulders. "Now Jake Morgan, my riding instructor, is suggesting I give her to my mother, with whom he says she's more compatible. He says I should get a quarter horse and ride western like Dad."

"He's right." Heath's words startled her, bringing

her attention back to him.

"What? How can you possibly come to that conclusion? You haven't seen me ride."

"I don't have to." He adjusted the sleeping bag around his shoulders. "I know freer in anything is what you need. That night you got soused on elderberry wine you were pretty terrific. That question about the oysters was almost more than a man could take and remain a gentleman."

"Oh, really? Aren't you the wise one."

She pulled a towel from a packsack and strode around behind him to begin drying his wet hair.

"Hey, dry it, don't remove it!"

She flung the towel aside and strode around in front of him, ready to continue their verbal battle, then unexpectedly laughed.

"What?" he asked squinting up at her in the sun.

"Somehow, with your hair sticking up in cowlicks and rooster tails, you don't quite cut the glorious movie-star image you're famous for."

"Image? Me? Who said I looked like a movie star? And which one? There are all kinds, all types."

"Careful, there. Your vanity is showing." *Damn, he was teasing.* With an exasperated sigh she turned away to get a cup of soup.

"I'm relieved the doe took her baby back," he said when she was seated across the fire from him. "I guess that blows away the old myth that a deer won't take her fawn back after it's been touched by a human."

"It also blew away another idea," she said, her gaze on her cup.

"Which is?" He set his soup aside, adjusted the sleeping bag about his shoulders, and looked at her.

"That you could have been involved in Gramps' death." She looked up to meet his gaze. "You could have let me jump into the river after that fawn. You knew I would have been drowned or died of hypothermia. With me out of the way through an accident, you'd probably have been able to have your way with the Chance."

"Thanks for the vote of confidence, but aren't you forgetting the infamous two percent?"

"No, but I've no doubt that, left on your own, you could finesse whoever it is."

"Nasty. And just when I thought we were on the verge of a lasting truce."

"One death-defying moment does not a peace treaty make. Come on, you must have some ideas."

"Someone wise and clear-sighted," he said. "Jack was too caring and clever to give such an important trust to just anyone else."

"But who?"

Heath shrugged. "It won't matter if you come to the right decision, will it?"

"And if I don't…in your opinion?"

"Then that wise, caring, third party will hold the deciding vote."

"Pretty confident, aren't you?" She finished her food and glanced over at him. "But then I guess you'd have to be, to risk criminal charges of, at the very least, forcible detainment by bringing me on this trip."

"I know Jack's fondest dream was that his Chance stay in his family. I'm not about to let that possibility die."

"Gramps told you that? Why didn't he tell me?"

"He wanted you to make your decision of your

own free will, not out of a sense of obligation."

"So why did you decide to tell me now?"

"You were willing to risk your life for that fawn. I don't need any further proof of your ability to care about what mattered to Jack. Now." He stood. "I'm going to get dressed in dry clothes here, where it's warm by the fire. Do you want to start setting up the tent? I'm sure Jack must have taught you how to do it. I don't plan to portage around these rapids until tomorrow."

"Portage?" Looking at the roiling water of the river below, she knew he was right. There was no possibility of passing through that section by canoe.

"Yes. You remember what that word means?"

"Of course I do…" He'd dropped his sleeping bag shroud. "Oh, for heaven's sake! Have a little modesty. And just for the book, you won't gain any points from being naked in front of me."

She swung away but not before she'd had a glimpse of broad shoulders, narrow hips, muscular thighs, and more. *Wow!* she thought as she struggled to set up the tent. *Heath Oakes, you're definitely a three-alarm wow.*

159

Chapter Ten

Sometime during the night, Allison awoke to the sensation of sharp cold on her face and the sound of something that sounded like pebbles hitting the canvas beside her.

"Snow." Heath's voice in the darkness answered her unvoiced question.

"What?!"

"Snow. A squall, not all that uncommon at this time of year. You'd know that if you'd ever visited the Chance in early May."

"Can't you ever give the guilt thing a rest? Lord, it's freezing!"

She heard him move. A moment later he was beside her.

"Come here." A zipper slithered.

"What?"

"Get inside with me." He drew her, sleeping bag and all, into his.

"Just a minute, mister..."

"What do you think I'm capable of doing with you swathed inside two layers of Thinsulate?"

"I...nothing...I don't know." The chuckle deep in his chest made her realize the foolishness of her protest.

"Warmer?"

"I suppose." She tried to sound indignant, but the sensations his warm, amazing body were producing tempered her attempt.

"Sleep." His lips brushed her temple, the word erotic in her ear. "And feel safe." He adjusted her vest pillow into a more comfortable position, pulled part of her sleeping bag into a hood about her head, then, with a sigh, settled once more for the night. As his regular breathing told Allison he slept, she suppressed the urge to reach out and run her fingers up that strong, clean-shaven jaw and into his soft golden-brown hair.

She'd never have been able to spend a platonic night with Paul. She remembered the unpleasant drive to the country club dance in the rain and Paul's unwelcome attempt at lovemaking that had caused the accident.

Lying in Heath Oakes' arms, she felt safe and secure. As she drifted off to sleep, a small, soft melody began to drift into her heart…

****

She awoke to a shock of chill air as Heath pulled away from her and arose. Sunlight peeked into their canvas shelter.

"Six o'clock." He pulled clean woolen socks from his packsack and sat down to replace the ones he'd slept in. "Rise and shine. I want you to see this morning before the sun melts the snow. It'll knock your socks off."

"I hope you're speaking figuratively." She climbed out of her sleeping bag and stretched. "Otherwise it could make for icy toes."

"Come on, come on!" He was lacing up his boots. "The snow won't last long in the sun."

He waited as she changed socks and laced on hiking boots. As she was pulling on her jacket, he caught her by the hand and drew her out into the dazzling day.

For a few seconds its brilliance blinded her, but as she became able to focus, a sigh of pure wonder escaped her lips. Virgin white covered grass, trees, and river shore, a pristine icing that sparkled with thousands of snow diamonds over layers of greenery glinting in the first golden rays of the sun. The panorama reminded Allison of a lady in a jade frock overlaid with jeweled lace. Except for the river thundering past, the wilderness seemed locked in a moment of absolute peace.

"It's fantastic!" she breathed.

"Wait. There's more." He took her hand and, pulling her along as eagerly as a child headed downstairs on Christmas morning, he led her up a slight incline to a place beneath a large birch tree several feet from their campsite. He knelt and brushed snow from some leaves disfigured with large brown spots. Moving them aside, he revealed a small clump of the most exquisite little blossoms Allison had ever seen.

"Mayflowers." She dropped to her knees. "I remember…"

"Smell them," he said, but when she leaned forward to pick one, he stopped her with a hand on her wrist.

"Just smell."

"Sorry. Forgot Gramps' no-picking rule." She bent and inhaled.

The scent from the tiny blossoms stirred wonderful memories. Light and yet intoxicatingly potent, she recalled it as the most exquisite fragrance she'd ever experienced.

"Heaven," she sighed, closing her eyes and inhaling from the bottom of her lungs. "The scent of mayflowers has to be a small piece of heaven."

"There's nothing quite like it," he said. "If someone could bottle it, they'd be a millionaire overnight. But no one ever has. Hopefully no one ever will. I want them to remain exactly what they are this moment—a unique, unspoiled bit of the wilderness."

"They will," she said dropping back on her knees. "I won't be selling out to National Realty."

She faced him as they knelt beside the bluish-tinged white blossoms. His expression of utter relief hit her straight in the heart.

"You mean it?" He got to his feet and squinted down at her in the sunlight.

"This place is your life, isn't it?"

"Yes." He turned to look out over the river sparkling dark and wild in the sun. "Jack Adams gave me a chance, and I plan to repay him by being the best steward I can to what he held important."

Allison got up and stood beside him. "*We'll* be the best stewards we can."

"What?"

"I'm staying. I'll handle the business aspect, and you'll take care of the outdoors component. What do you say?"

"What about Toronto, your CFO job?"

"I did a lot of thinking last night. I decided I don't want to spend my life working for someone else, helping make someone's big business even bigger. The important stuff is all here."

Before she could protest, he had her in his arms and was kissing her, kissing her until she swirled away into some wonderful place where her body melted into his, where reality was only his hard body and the sound of the river and his heart thudding against hers. But when she wrapped her arms about his neck and started to come full-length against him, he stopped her, drew her out from him, and looked deep into her expectant green eyes.

"No."

"What...no? Heath, why..."

"Believe me, I'm not pulling back because I want to." He cupped her face in his hands. "But I made a promise to your mother that I'd 'be a gentleman,' to use her euphemism, for the whole of any time I spent alone on the Chance with you."

"Heath..."

"Allie, this isn't easy for me. God knows, I'd like nothing better than to make love to you right now, this minute. But you could end up regretting it, and I don't want that to happen...again."

"I won't, I wouldn't..."

"But I would. Let's get portaging...while I'm still able to."

He released her and headed back toward their campfire.

"Heath!" She caught up to him and grabbed his arm.

"Hey, look, I promised your mother I'd keep things platonic, and that's the way they'll stay!" He swung on her. "I got carried away when you told me you weren't going to sell the Chance, that you'd be staying. I'm sorry. But I'm not made of steel. Believe me, beneath the surface still beats the heart of the same guy you had to fight off when you were a romantic teenager. But we have to take it slow and see where it goes. We're not kids anymore. This could get serious. Come on. Let's get packing…Allie."

****

"I hear you calling when we part, this river flows through both our hearts…"

"What's that you're singing?" He stopped beside her as she packed supplies into a cooler.

"Something I heard Gramps sing to Gram." She straightened and faced him squarely. "Could be something that happened recently reminded me of it."

"The man must have been in love with her." He turned away and began to gather their tent and rolled-up sleeping bags.

"Must have been." She cast him a sidewise glance.

"Look, if you're expecting some kind of commitment from me…"

"Of course not. One hot kiss does not a commitment make. Or a business arrangement."

She returned to packing, something like heartburn nagging her chest.

He threw the bundles onto his shoulder and headed for the canoe.

An hour later they'd loaded the canoe on a small set of wheels and packed all their gear in it except for one well-filled large packsack.

"Let me help you with this." Heath picked it up and turned to Allison.

"Do I look like a pack mule?" she asked, her eyes widening.

"I can't pull all our gear and the canoe over the rough terrain up ahead. So unless you want to wait alone at the other end of the portage while I make two trips, you'll have to carry your own stuff. Or aren't you up to it?" His eyes challenged her.

"Strap it on, buddy." She turned her back to him and waited. "I'm Jack Adams' granddaughter, remember?"

He slipped the straps over her shoulders, but as she fastened the chest support, he leaned around the side of the pack to place a kiss on her temple.

"Remind me never again to promise Myra Armstrong I'll remain celibate around her daughter," he muttered. He took up the straps to pull the canoe. "Right now I'd rather live up to my uninhibited wild man persona."

"That image gets foggier by the minute. A genuine lord of the jungle—er, woods—would heft this little bitty canoe over his head, packsack on his back, and stride off into the bush, resting it on his manly shoulders, the woman walking proud and unburdened by his side."

"You left out the fact that his woman probably would be scantily clad." He started off with the canoe in tow. "That might inspire a man to give it his best shot."

They were battling their way up a rocky promontory above the river twenty minutes later when an explosion rent the quiet of the forest. Heath dropped the canoe straps and dove at Allison. Together they crashed to the ground. The freed canoe bounced down the slope, splashed into the river, and bounded away in the current.

"Ah, hell!"

"Ouch…Heath, you're crushing me. What…"

"Lie still!" Heath hissed. "That was a rifle shot!"

"What? Someone is shooting at us?"

"Yeah, *someone*. No bear, no sasquatch. A real person. Start edging behind those rocks. Whoever he is, he's back in the trees. If we can get over the lip of the cliff and down under it, we have a chance."

"A chance? Wasn't that an accident? A hunting mistake?"

"In May? Hunting season starts in October. Now crawl…fast…like a crab." She obeyed, scuttling over rocks and moss until she dropped over the edge of the cliff above the river. A split second later Heath landed beside her with a grunt.

"Keep your head down and follow me." He started off over the shedding shale of the high river ledge, stooped like a handsome Quasimodo.

Allison glanced down at the river roaring below them and shuddered. One wrong step and she'd be following their canoe over rocks and rapids.

Praying and crossing her fingers, she scrambled after Heath, the packsack threatening to destroy her equilibrium. At one point she slipped, the loose rock crumbling under her boots. Only Heath's hand grabbing her shoulder strap saved her from tumbling down into the rapids. With a gasp she righted herself and scrambled after him.

"In here." He caught her hand to pull her into a dark hole under a ledge.

"Phew! What's that awful stench?"

The smell engulfed her as they came to a crouching stop in the blackness.

"Quiet," he muttered. "This is a bear den."

"Are you crazy?" She leaped upright, hit her head, and fell back rubbing it. "What if he comes home?

What if he…?"

"He won't. He's too busy looking for food. Anyway, hiding here beats the hell out of dodging bullets."

"Frying pan or fire." She hunkered down with a pounding heart and a sore spot on her head. "How long do you reckon we'll have to stay here?"

"Until dusk. Then we'll sneak back up over the ledge and find a safe place for the night. Your sleeping bag is in your pack, as well as a frying pan and a pot. We'll manage."

"An empty frying pan and an empty pot," she breathed, the full extent of their predicament washing over her. "Miles from civilization with our canoe, food, and ninety percent of our camping gear gone."

"Not to panic. Remember you're with the Lord of the Woods. He and his woman always survive. They have to. Otherwise there'd be no more movies." In the darkness he slipped an arm about her sagging shoulders and planted a kiss on her taut lips. "Relax and enjoy the ambience. Quite a different aroma from those mayflowers but still just as natural."

"Very amusing. You said someone was deliberately shooting at us, but who? Why?"

"I'm not sure who, but I do know why. To coerce us into selling the Chance to National Realty."

"National Realty? I find that hard to believe. They're legitimate realtors with branches right across Canada."

"Are you saying big business isn't capable of using underhanded methods? I know you're a member of their rank and file, but still you can't believe that crock."

"No, but I…"

"And exactly what do we know about this James Wilcox who's supposedly their agent?"

"Well, about the man, nothing, actually. What makes you say 'supposedly'?"

"The fact that he's yet to produce any ID that identifies him as one of their full-time employees. And the fact that these so-called sasquatch sightings became much more frequent once he began trying to buy the Chance. My opinion is that he's a freelancer working on a commission basis."

For a few minutes they sat in silence. Then Allison spoke.

"Heath, Candace Breckenridge alluded to a scare she got when she was up here last fall. Did she see the sasquatch?"

"Is that what she said?" A sneer colored his words.

"Well, she gave some story about almost being caught with you by her husband, but since you've told me there was never anything between you…"

"There never was." He let out an exasperated sigh. "But it looked as if there was, when her husband found her with me in my bedroom."

"In your bedroom? And you're telling me your relationship with her was purely platonic? Ouch!" She'd tried to jump to her feet and banged her head…again.

"Take it easy. Let me explain. Jack and the other guides took the guests downriver on a picnic. Mom went along to serve lunch. I thought I was alone in the Lodge area. I didn't know the Breckenridges had had a fight and stayed behind. I hadn't had a day off in weeks, so I decided to take a shower, go into town, and convince Jesse to have lunch with me."

"Ah, ha! So you and Dr. Henderson are…were…"

"Friends. Don't jump up again. I had just gone into my bedroom to dress when Candace burst into the cottage screaming something about seeing a big hairy ape down near the boathouse. Claimed it was a sasquatch. Before I could stop her, she threw herself at me, and toppled me backwards onto the bed. She knocked the towel from my hips and when her husband, drawn by her screams, arrived, you can guess what he thought he was seeing."

"You mean Robert Breckenridge saw you lying on your bed buff naked with his wife sprawled over you and he didn't try to kill you?" Allison gasped. "Wow! If my father had caught you with my mother like that, your hide would currently be nailed to the boathouse door."

"I don't intend ever to be in that position with his wife." Heath's voice was teasing, sensuous. "But with his daughter…I have a healthy imagination and high hopes."

"Dream on." But she smiled in the darkness. Then she sucked in her breath as a thought stuck her. "Heath, you don't suppose that's Robert Breckenridge out there shooting at us?"

"Hardly. He was one of the poorest woodsmen I've ever encountered. He loved to fish, but his guide even had to bait his hook. I doubt he'd know how to fire a rifle."

"Was that the first reported sasquatch sighting?"

"First one I'd ever heard of."

"Poor Candace." Allison was thoughtful. "Dad claims her husband's only passion is Triam Industries.

As long as he and Candace stay married and he remains in control of the company, he couldn't care less what his wife does."

"I felt sorry for her." Heath exhaled a weary sigh. "He managed to ignore her completely even up here on vacation. As a result, I included her in the canoe trips I was guiding while he went off fishing with Jack. She became quite adept at camping and told me she'd been a champion skeet shooter in her teens, even suggested Jack put in a facility for it. Can you imagine Jack installing a shooting gallery? He was so anti-guns there isn't a single one on the place, sasquatch or no sasquatch."

"And she fell in love with you," Allison finished.

"I wouldn't describe her interest in me as love."

"Oh, dear."

"Yeah, oh, dear. At the time, I would have denied that fact. After all, the woman is almost old enough to be my mother. But then, just before she and her husband were to leave to return to Toronto, she came to see me down at the boathouse. She said that if I could convince Jack to sell the Chance, she'd buy it—at a generous price, mind you—and put me in full charge. I thought she was talking a lot of nonsense. Now I'm beginning to believe she meant every word."

"Another CEO under her control," Allison muttered. "Or, more accurately, a bought-and-paid-for lover in their own secluded love nest."

"I guess." He moved in the darkness, and Allison sensed the discomfort the honesty of their discussion was causing him.

"Of course, Gramps refused."

"Right. But within days the mythical sasquatch

171

first sighted by Candace began to put in regular appearances to the wives and children of our guests. After that, business began to fall off."

"Surely you don't think Candace is impersonating that thing?"

"She was safely back in Toronto. But with her kind of money, people can be hired to do just about anything. The question is who."

"And can we manage to elude him until we get back to civilization? Why is it taking us so long to travel by water from the Chance to Adams' Landing? By road it's an hour's drive."

"The North Passage horseshoes between those two points," he said. "It loops far back into the wilderness, winding and twisting for miles. The road runs as the crow flies."

"What point on this horseshoe do you think we've reached?"

"We've come over the top and are about one third of the way down the other side...one good solid day's walk from the Landing. Nowhere near a difficult hike if we didn't have to worry about whoever is out there trying to make trophies of us."

Chapter Eleven

"This is cozy." Allison snuggled against Heath's shoulder. "No one could possibly find us under all these branches."

She looked up at the huge spruce towering above them, its wide lower limbs spreading out to form a thick, arched canopy over them before bending gracefully down to touch their tips to the ground and conceal the couple.

"They will if you don't keep your voice down." He quieted her with a kiss that left a warm feeling of invitation coursing through her.

"Remarkable." Allison snuggled closer and sighed.

"Not nearly as remarkable as I am," he muttered against her hair, "spending the night sharing a sleeping bag with you and remaining celibate."

"You promised Mom, remember?"

She put a finger lightly to his lips and smiled in the darkness, admiring his integrity and hating it all at the same time. "As for anyone finding us, I don't see how that's humanly possible. After we left that bear den, we traveled miles away from the river, backtracking and circling and jumping across brooks before we ended up back on its banks again."

"You forget…whoever is on our case is obviously an experienced woodsman. We can't be too careful."

"Okay, okay." She adjusted herself against him

again and lowered her voice to a near whisper. "Heath, tell me about you...about your life before you came to live with my grandfather. You know everything about me, and I know so little about you."

"Not much to tell. My grandmother was a war bride. She'd run away from home to marry a Canadian soldier, and her parents apparently had nothing to do with her after that. She came to this country with my grandfather after the war. Shortly after they arrived in Canada and settled in Halifax, my mother was born. Not long after that, my grandparents were killed in a boating accident."

"Heath, I'm sorry."

"I'm sorry I didn't have a chance to know them." Regret seeped into his voice. "My mother was sent to live with an uncle and his wife. They already had six children and weren't anxious for another, but they took her in since she had no other place to go. She grew up feeling unloved and unwanted. When, at seventeen, she met my father, she married him within a couple of months. I think she'd finally found all the love that had been missing from her life. At least, that's what I gathered listening to her talk about my father."

He paused and Allison stroked his cheek. "Go on."

"He was a high steel worker...bridges, high-rises, that sort of thing. I was born ten months after they were married. Two days after their first anniversary, my dad slipped and fell from where he was working on the bridge over Halifax Harbor. He died instantly. My mother, with little education, no family to help her, and next to no money, was left alone to raise me."

"Oh, Heath..."

"I never knew my father, so I never missed him."

He cleared his throat. "But it was hard for my mother. She took any job she could get—waitress, cook, dishwasher. We must have moved a dozen times before I was twelve, each time to a cheaper and poorer apartment in a rougher section of the city. Things just seemed to get harder and harder...for both of us. The whole thing came to a boil when I stole that car and racked it up."

He paused, and Allison sensed the emotions roiling inside him.

"Heath, that girl...that Jennifer...what she did, it would have driven anyone a little crazy," she said softly.

"Hardly a valid reason for what I did. At least, that's what Jack said. A couple of months after I was sentenced, my mother saw an ad in a maritime daily newspaper. Someone with a wilderness lodge in New Brunswick was looking for a cook/housekeeper. She decided to apply, hoping she'd get the job but worried sick she would have to leave me incarcerated in Halifax. She saw only one way to do it. She applied telling Jack the truth about her circumstances. When she had no answer in over a week, she decided he wasn't interested. Imagine her surprise when he showed up at our apartment one June afternoon and asked her how soon she and her son could be ready to go with him back to New Brunswick. Seems he'd already spent a couple of days at the Justice Department getting me placed in his custody so I could leave the province with them."

"Gramps was one amazing man."

"I wasn't much of a joy to either of them after I came to live here. I tried to run away a couple of times.

175

The first time Jack caught me and brought me back, he was reasoning and understanding; the second time he threatened the bejeebers out of me, which was exactly what I needed."

"And so you reformed."

"Started to. Then you and your mother arrived. I think I might have managed to stay away from you, but you had that big, obvious crush on me..."

"Now just a minute, Mr. Macho..."

"Do you deny it?"

Silence. Then, reluctantly, "No. But still..."

"You reminded me of Jennifer—pretty, and rich, and stuck-up."

"I wasn't...stuck up."

"Sure, you were. You got everything you wanted. And that summer you wanted romance with a bad boy."

"Oh, God."

"True, isn't it?"

"I guess, but it embarrasses me to hear it."

"Okay, moving on. We had that incident, and you went away. Jack must have suspected something, because after you left he called me down to the boathouse, lifted me off my feet by the front of my jacket, and told me that if he ever found out any part of me had touched his granddaughter, he'd amputate it."

" Gramps wouldn't hurt anything—"

"Anything that didn't threaten his granddaughter. From his expression that day I wasn't about to risk another encounter with you. But I didn't have to worry. You never came back."

The soft sounds of the wilderness filled the following wordless moments. An owl hooted, a coyote howled, frogs chirped.

"Heath?"

"Hmmm?" He nuzzled her hair.

"Were you sorry…that I didn't come back?"

"Sorry and relieved. I wanted to see you again, to make things right between us, but relieved that I wouldn't be tempted to do anything that could lead to bodily mutilation."

She felt the soft chuckle in his chest and smiled into the darkness.

"In that case, so am I. I really like you…intact."

"Don't tease. We have to get some sleep."

He settled against her. She tried to relax and follow suit. It wasn't easy. Lying beneath that huge spruce, its spicy fragrance adding to the sensuousness of the star-sparkled night in the arms of this earthy man, was almost more than she could bear. Heath's long muscular body wrapped about hers made her heart race, her senses catapult. She longed to run her hands up under his shirt, to feel those hard ripples of flesh with her fingers, to kiss his lips, his neck, the hollow at his shoulder.

His regular breathing told her he slept. She drew a deep breath, forced down the quiver threatening to rush through her body, and struggled for sleep. Fifteen miles with five thousand two hundred and eighty feet in each. Or was it one thousand seven hundred and sixty yards? How many feet…yards…?

She awoke to sunlight winking into her eyes between the branches. She blinked, struggled up on one elbow, and realized she was alone in the sleeping bag.

"Heath?" Panic seized her. "Heath?"

"Not so loud. We don't want to let the wrong people know where we are. Come out and have some eggs."

She crawled on hands and knees from their sleeping shelter and saw him near the riverbank. The thin trickle of smoke from a small fire drifted off across the river on a lazy breeze.

"Eggs?" She struggled to her feet, stiff from a night on hard ground. "Where did you get eggs?"

"Partridge. Big nest on the ground over there. I counted fourteen."

"You robbed some poor bird's nest?" Allison rubbed her eyes and looked down at the panful of scrambled eggs bubbling on the fire.

"No choice." He hunkered down and stirred them with a stick. "We need nourishment. She won't mind…much. Partridge often have up to three hatches a year."

"And you had matches?" She pointed to the fire.

"I'd be a pretty poor woodsman if I didn't have some in a waterproof container on me. Sit. These are almost ready."

"What about the smoke? Aren't you afraid someone might see it?"

"It's drifting off across the river, away from anyone on this side who might be on our trail. It'll dissipate fast over water. Ditto for any faint scent of cooking. At any rate, we have to risk it. We need nourishment, it's too early in the season for nuts and berries, and I'm not feral enough to eat raw eggs."

"And what's for lunch? Some poor, dead animal?" She tried to be critical of what he'd done but realized he'd had little choice. She also realized she was ravenous.

"Let me surprise you." He took the frying pan from

the fire, using the sleeve of his shirt pulled over his hand as protection from the heat.

He dropped the pan between them and handed her a piece of bark he'd fashioned into a crude spoon.

"Eat," he said and picked up a similar utensil.

She did and found she was even hungrier than she'd thought.

"Tea?" he asked when they'd cleaned the pan, eating scoop for scoop.

"Don't tease."

"I'm not. Raspberry leaves boiled make a strong, nourishing brew. Here, try it."

He picked up the pot from where it had been cooling beside the fire and handed it to her.

Gingerly she raised it to her lips and took a sip of the bitter, bracing brew. She coughed, then took another drink.

"It won't replace Starbucks," she said, handing it to him, "but it does have a get-going kick."

"That's what we need right now." Heath took a long drink, handed the pot back to her, and stood. "You're staring. Egg on my face or what?"

"No, just a good healthy stubble. A further crack in your heroic mystique. A jungle movie hero, for instance, never sports a stubble, no matter how long he's in the bush with his loincloth as his only luggage."

"Sorry my whiskers have shattered the last of your fantasies. Let's get packing. It might not be healthy to stay too long in one place in daylight."

"I have to wash my face." Allison got to her feet and headed down to the bank of the river.

She squatted by the river, splashed icy water over her face, pulled out her shirttail to dry it, and suddenly chuckled. Was she the same woman who only a few days earlier had thought ruining her designer suit a major disaster? Now here she was in bush gear she seemed to have been wearing forever, her hair such a tangle she could barely finger comb it, washing her face in a wilderness river, using her shirttail for a towel. She wondered what Paul Bradley would think of her and then laughed out loud because she didn't care.

"Come on, Allie. Let's get going." Brought out of her daydreams by his call, she started back to where he was waiting, fire extinguished, packsack on his back. She had never felt so alive, so ready for whatever adventure would challenge them.

The terrain they traveled that morning varied. Sometimes their way was along a low riverbank close to a smoothly flowing stretch of water. At others, they climbed over rocks high above rapids and gorges where the river swirled and roiled like a thing possessed.

When they paused to rest at noon, it was in a gently sloping meadow that ended in a cluster of alders at the water's edge. The bright sun and clear skies of early morning had vanished behind a low cloud cover, and a fog had begun to roll in. Together they gathered dry branches, and Heath lighted a small fire on the river's edge.

"Sit here and rest." He stood and turned to her. "I'll find lunch."

"I can't wait to see what you come up with this time. I'm so hungry almost anything you deem edible will be accepted."

He narrowed his eyes, pulled his knife from its scabbard, and ran his finger along its blade.

"Heath, no! Not some animal!"

"Hand me the cooking pot, there. I'm off to harvest nuts and berries."

"It's too early in the season." She caught the teasing in his tone and knelt to open the packsack. "Although I said I could eat almost anything, I'm not fond of twigs and roots."

"Noted. Avoid roots and twigs."

He took the pot and headed off into the fog toward the alders along the river. Allison adjusted the pack into a headrest, lay down, and stretched out to wait. Weary after an arduous morning, she dozed. For how long, she couldn't be sure. But she was certain that when she awoke it was with a feeling of being watched.

"Heath?" She jerked to a sitting position. The fog had thickened. She could see no more than a few feet in any direction. "Heath, is that you?" Her words sounded hollow and eerie.

There was no answer, but something moved a few yards away in the veil of whiteness.

"Heath?"

The answer was a grunt. A huge, hulking, hairy creature materialized out of the mist. It shambled toward her, hirsute hands extended toward her throat.

"Heath!" Allison stumbled to her feet, grabbed the packsack and started at a dead run in the direction in which he'd gone.

When she slammed into the hard wall of his chest, he caught her in his arms.

"Allie, what…?"

"Sasquatch! Back there!"

"Wait here." He moved her aside, pulled his knife, and headed into the mist.

She stood trembling. Silence returned to the mist.

Its surreal ambience and the memory of the monster that had threatened her made her stomach churn. Time moved like a slug. Finally she decided she couldn't wait passively any longer. What if the creature had attacked Heath, overpowered him? Maybe at that very minute, the hairy giant was throttling the life out of him. She had to find some way to help. An inspiration took hold. She remembered the fire Heath had lighted on the riverbank near where she'd fallen asleep. *Animals are afraid of fire. If I get back to the fire, I can help Heath...*

Keeping the river to her left, she started back downstream. When she finally found the fire site, she was so relieved she barely noticed the pot of greens bubbling over the flames. Grabbing a stick, she thrust it into the coals and waited. If that thing came back, all she had to do was pull out her torch and, hopefully, he'd flee in fear. Hopefully.

Hugging her bent knees, she hunkered down beside the fire and waited and hoped and prayed. What was taking Heath so long? Since no sounds of a struggle rent the silence, she could only assume he hadn't accosted the creature. But then maybe the thing had gotten behind him, struck him down without a sound. Maybe Heath was lying somewhere out there in the fog—wounded, dying, dead! *Oh, dear God, let him be all right.*

"Lunch ready?" Grinning, he stepped out of the mist. Relief flooded through her with strength-sapping force. She tried to get to her feet but stumbled and fell, unable to make her knees support her.

"Allie!" He squatted in front of her and put his hands on her shoulders. "Whatever it was, it's gone."

"What was it?" She collapsed against his shoulder.

"Some guy in a Halloween costume." He kissed her mist-dampened hair. "Ran like a rabbit before I could get a good look at him. We're okay for now, but I think we'd better eat up and get moving."

"You don't believe what I saw was a sasquatch?" She stared up at him.

"No, not a sasquatch. Someone sent to scare us, maybe do us actual physical harm if that scare doesn't work." His tone lightened as he pulled her to her feet with him. "Come on. I've cooked up one of nature's truly exotic dishes, available fresh for only two weeks of the year. I came back while you were sleeping and started them boiling. I went back to look for more but couldn't find any. I was returning when Hairy Harry decided to give you nightmares."

He swung about on his haunches and used a stick to lift the pot from its place above the flames. With a triumphant grin, he set the steaming dish in front of her.

"What is it?" She looked into the bubbling greenery. "Spinach?"

"Fiddleheads." He drained off the water. "Immature ferns. They look like the head of a fiddle, thus the name. Try some."

He handed her a pronged twig and grinned.

"You're really quite adept at making unique utensils," she said. "Maybe guests at the Lodge might enjoy them…the crowning touch of their wilderness experience."

"Maybe." He reached out and ran his knuckles lightly down her cheek. The expression in his eyes upped her heartbeat to way past the speed limit.

"You know, Heath Oakes, I'm getting a tad fond of

you." The admittance was soft, almost shy.

"Just fond?" He drew her into his arms. The next moment he was kissing her, kissing her until her feet left the ground, until all she was conscious of was him, his mouth, his body. "Just fond?" He raised his head to look down into her eyes with his amazing ones that narrowed when he was intense.

"Maybe more than fond." He kissed her again, his tongue tasting, probing, and when he looked at her again, she could only breathe, "Oh, yes, definitely more than fond."

"If I hadn't promised your mother…" His words tickled her ear as his hands slid down her back.

"Heath." His name was a breathed permission, a sensuous request.

"No, no, no." He threw up his hands and backed off. "Hell, no. I'm a fool, but I do keep my word."

"You pick the damnedest moments to get all trustworthy and righteous." Frustrated, she jerked away from him.

"Sorry. But I never promised anything once we're out of this mess and back on equal footing. I don't think Myra, who married a cowboy, will expect her daughter to keep her own maverick waiting too long."

"Great, good, wonderful. Let's get going."

****

It was nearing dusk when they reached Adams Landing and headed up across the field toward the tombstone looming out of the fog.

"We made it…" Allison began. A deafening roar and a rifle bullet ricocheting off her grandparents' headstone cut her short.

The next instant she was flat on the ground behind

184

it. Heath's body pinned her to the earth. *Damn it, déjà vous!*

"Don't move!" he hissed.

As if I could. His body giving her no alternative, Allison lay still and felt his heart pounding against her back.

"Stay close to the headstone." Barely audible, his words fell into her ear.

"Heath…"

"Stay!"

He eased away from her, catlike, into the fog. Alone, with her heart trying to hammer its way out of her chest, Allison lay with her fingers clutching the base of her grandparents' tombstone and prayed.

Time became a dragging, wretched thing, its passing an excruciating endurance test. Then a voice made Allison start so violently she felt her shoulders snap.

"Get up!"

She turned and looked up to find the long barrel of a rifle pointed at her head. The woman holding it was Candace Breckenridge, dressed in camouflage bush gear.

"Candace!" She stumbled to her feet. "What…?"

"You spoiled brat!" she snarled, and Allison felt her blood turn to ice water as she saw the insane rage in the woman's face. "You think your grandfather left you a lover in his will, don't you? That you own Heath Oakes just like you own this land? Well, think again, honey. A sexy little body like yours might be okay on a camping trip, but it takes money to keep the fire burning three hundred and sixty-five days a year. Heath Oakes knows that. He also knows that while your daddy

185

might be rich, that doesn't necessarily mean you are. But he damn well knows I am! He might exude all the trappings of a gorgeous savage, but remember where he came from and what he still is under all that earthy charm."

"You can't buy people!" From somewhere Allison found the courage to snap back.

"That's what you think. Heath has a taste for money and is willing to do whatever it takes to get it. He got rid of old Jack and seduced that doctor into signing the death certificate, no questions asked. He'll convince her to do the same with you after the unfortunate accident you're about to have. Once we're rid of you, Heath and I will turn your grandfather's Chance into a sure thing...and have our own private love nest."

"That will never happen." *I have to keep her talking until Heath gets back. It's my only chance.*

"Sorry to disappoint you, sweetie, but it will. That fool Jim Wilcox may have failed in doing what I paid him to do, but I won't! Heath Oakes is still a kid from the slums, out to grab the golden ring at the first opportunity. Within a week, both he and this place will be all mine, and you'll be a distant memory."

The woman raised the rifle to her shoulder, eased back on the trigger, and aimed at the younger woman's chest.

Allison looked into the face of death.

Chapter Twelve

Out of the fog leaped a creature, a hairy, dirty creature that hit Candace Breckenridge in mid-back and sent her face forward onto the ground. *Oh, God, a baby sasquatch!* The rifle discharged up into the fog, then flew from Candace's hands to skitter across the wet grass toward Allison.

Amid the woman's cries to get the thing off her, Allison grabbed the gun and stumbled to her feet.

"Jack!" The dog's name was a gasp as she recognized the animal standing on the woman's back and stilling her efforts with vicious growls and rolled-back lips.

"What the…?" Heath burst out of the fog. His eyes widened. "Sweet Jesus, what's going on?"

"Jack appeared out of nowhere and saved my life." Allison handed the gun to the man as he came to stand beside her. "She was going to shoot me."

"Get this miserable thing off me!" Candace cried. She tried to rise, but Jack grabbed a mouthful of her hair and yanked her back into submission.

"It's okay, boy." Allison stepped forward to take the dog's collar and pull him, protesting, off the woman. "But thank you, thank you, thank you." She knelt and hugged the filthy animal, whose coat offered no evidence of its former snowy whiteness. Muddy and tangled, he did resemble a small sasquatch.

"Here." Heath pulled off his belt and tossed it to Allison. "Tie her hands behind her back."

"Stupid, ignorant, backwoods garbage!" Candace raged. "You could have had it all!"

"Get something I can use to tie her up with from our pack, Allie." He thrust the woman against the grave marker as Allison finished her task. "Just to be sure she'll stay available until we can contact the RCMP."

Her hands suddenly shaking, her knees threatening to desert her, Allison did as instructed. When she handed a plaid shirt to him, his expression mirrored remorse and tenderness.

"All this was my fault, Allie," he muttered, taking it from her. "None of this would have happened to you if..."

"Heath, what she said about you and her..."

"Fantasies." He wrapped the material around Candace's ankles and pulled it tight.

"Fantasies?!" Candace Breckenridge screamed at him. "Moonlight strolls, drinks in front of the fire, talking for hours over breakfast coffee... You call all that fantasies?" The woman glared at him. "You're a backwoods gigolo, Heath Oakes. I hope you make this little bitch as miserable as you've made me."

"Heath! Heath! Where are you?" Marty Mason's voice echoed eerily out of the fog.

"Over here." Heath stood from his task. "By Jack's grave."

Jack muttered a growl. "It's okay, boy." Allison held his collar and spoke reassuringly.

Mason and his three buddies from the service station appeared out of the mist. The former's bearded face relaxed when he saw the restrained woman on the ground.

"Thank God!" he muttered and drew the back of his hand across his mouth. "This woman," he indicated Candace, "Stole my ATV and my deer rifle. Told me I was fired, that she'd finish the job herself."

"Fired?" Allison stared at the man. "Fired from what?"

"She hired me to play sasquatch and ruin the Lodge's business so she could buy it cheap and easy." He avoided her eyes. "A few days ago, when she called to see how things were goin', I told her I'd heard from a couple of guys who were mindin' the Lodge that you and Heath were gone down river campin' for a few days. She got real upset and offered me a lot of money to dog you two along the trip, shake you up with sasquatch sightings, a few shots over your heads, and the like." He turned to the man holding the rifle. "I really needed that money, Heath."

"Leaving us without our gear was a notch or two above scaring," Heath muttered. "We might have died."

"Ah, Heath, you know I wouldn't have let that happen. I called the Mounties after I accidentally knocked you off the boathouse roof. I only planned to take the ladder and leave you stuck up there for a while, or force you to jump into the river to get down. I was mad as hell for you sackin' me. But now, serious hurtin' or killin'? You know I wouldn't do anything like that."

"You were with me when we saw the sasquatch on the road to the Chance." Allison looked at the man.

"That was me," one of his companions admitted. "Marty set me up to do it while you were in the service station, when he said he had to gas up his Jeep."

"But this woman," Allison pointed at Candace Breckenridge, "was going to use your rifle to murder me!" She swung back on Marty Mason.

"She stole it, I tell you! She came to my place around noon. I was just getting back from giving you that last scare. I'd traveled pretty fast, had my ATV hidden in the bush. She questioned me about what I'd done, how shook up you'd been by my tactics. When I made some crack about scarin' the two of you right into each other's arms, she went crazy. Said she was takin' the four-wheeler and my deer rifle back into the bush to check on the situation. Man, right then I got a sick feeling. I told her no way and turned my back on her.

"She must have hit me with something, because the next thing I knew I woke up face down in my driveway. The ATV and my rifle that was strapped to the back of it were gone." He licked dry lips and wiped sweat from his forehead before he continued, "I figured you'd be gettin' near Adams Landing, so I called my buddies to come with me. Just when we were ready to start out, Jamie arrived. Said he and Carl had lost that blasted dog, that it had run off early yesterday morning and they needed us to help find it."

"Jamie and Carl?"

"The two men I had taking care of Jack and the Lodge." Heath's explanation was quick and terse. "Go on, Marty."

"We agreed to keep our eyes open for the mutt, but right then I was more concerned about *her*," he pointed to Candace, "And what she might do with that rifle."

"I believe you, Marty." Heath hefted the rifle onto his shoulder. "She could have gotten here on her own, given all the information she gleaned from me during our canoe trips last summer. She was an excellent student. Now let's get her to the police. Allie and Jack and I are hungry and tired and cold and...really dirty." He looked down at the young woman holding the dog, grinned, and wiped something she guessed was mud from her cheek.

****

Two hours later, when they got out of the RCMP Jeep that had driven them back to the Lodge, a couple burst from the front door to greet them.

"Mom! Dad!" Allison cried as Myra and Cameron Armstrong came down the steps to greet them.

"We decided we'd better come and see for ourselves how you were making out." Dr. Armstrong watched as his wife embraced their daughter. "Your mother was getting a little concerned about the deal she'd made with Heath, and I don't blame her. If she'd let me in on her scheme to make you appreciate the Chance, I would have nipped it in the bud. Apparently it was one rough voyage, judging from your appearance. The police presence alone is worthy of a detailed explanation. Good God, Jack, what happened to you?"

"He's a hero." Allison went from her mother's arms to her father's. "I'll tell you all about it later. Right now I'm tired and cold and hungry...and, like Jack, really dirty."

The Lodge door opened again. Paul Bradley emerged, cleanly shaved, every hair in place, wearing black pants and gray silk shirt. He had his cell phone pressed to his ear.

"Al!" He punched an end to his call and came down the steps. He started to take her into his arms as

191

her father released her, then stopped short. "Damn it, you're filthy!"

Jack muttered something unpleasant.

"Business as usual?" Allison stepped back and indicated the phone in his hand.

"Just checking in at the office. You're really disheveled, hon."

"She's had a rough time." Heath spoke from several feet behind her.

"Really? And what part did you play in it, buddy?" Paul swung to confront the dirty, bearded man.

"Paul, please…" Allison tried to intervene, but he pushed her aside.

"No, no, I have a right to know."

"A lot happened to us these last few days." Heath looked down at him, eyes narrowing in the feral cat look Allison had come to recognize as dangerous. "But nothing that would sully your…relationship…if there really is one. Is there, Allie?"

"No." Her reply was abrupt and definite.

"Al, what are you saying?" Paul turned to her. "You can't possibly prefer this dirty backwoods savage."

"That's exactly what I am saying, Paul. I plan to stay here and help him keep Gramps' Chance intact."

"You've got to be kidding. Give up a job as a top executive at one of Canada's fastest growing corporations? You'd have to be crazy."

"Maybe I am. Crazy like Gramps. Crazy like a fox." She smiled up at Heath. "Anyhow, I'm going to give it my best shot."

"Argh!" Paul looked down as Jack raised his leg and peed down the sharp crease of his trousers. "Filthy creature! I don't know how you can tolerate him, Myra."

Shaking his leg every few steps, he headed back into the Lodge.

"You're sure about this, Allison?" Her mother's smooth forehead wrinkled into a frown. "It's a big decision."

"It's what Gramps...and you...were hoping for, isn't it? Furthermore, I'm quite sure I know who holds those two controlling shares."

"Really?" Myra crossed her arms on her chest as her husband, grinning, put an arm around her shoulders. "Who?"

"Well, you have one." Allison tried to look clever and sly all at once. "And Heath's mother has the other."

"When did you come to that conclusion?" Myra Armstrong held her ground.

"Oh, come on, Mom. Who else could it be? One dependable person from each of the opposing camps."

"And just when did you figure this out?" Heath, his forehead furrowing, stared at her .

"It came to me in one giant epiphany right after Candace shot at us. Hitting the ground with you on top of me knocked away the cobwebs."

"Hitting the ground with..." Cameron Armstrong's arm dropped from about his wife and he faced Heath with a look Allison knew boded no good.

"Heath was pushing me out of the way of a bullet." Allison took her father's arm and looked up at him, grinning. "Dad, really. I'm a woman now. I can handle this guy with one hand tied behind my back." She shot Heath a taunting look.

"Maybe." She felt her father's muscles relax. "But

since you're going to be staying up here with him, I'll repeat the warning Jack told me he gave you many years ago. Any part of you that touches my daughter without her heartfelt permission will be amputated. As a surgeon, I'm perfectly capable of carrying out the threat."

"Understood, sir." Heath stepped forward and held out his hand.

"Good." Dr. Armstrong accepted the offer, and the two men stood grinning at each other.

"Good Lord!" Allison linked arms with her mother. "I'm starting to feel like mere chattel. Let's go inside. I'm hoping you'll make tea and sandwiches while I take a shower and try to get back to being human."

"Jack, you'd better come along with me." Cameron Armstrong looked down at the dog. "I think a good bath is in order before you're fit for the Lodge."

Jack looked up at him and barked.

"Okay, okay, I know how you feel about baths, but we guys all have to do things we don't particularly like, to please the ladies." He turned to the younger man. "Remember that, Heath. Because, if you're not already, I think you're about to become involved with one very special one."

Chapter Thirteen

"Bye, see you soon." The following day Allison waved as her parents drove off in the Tracker they'd rented in town on their arrival. Paul had left in a huff shortly after she and Heath arrived back at the Lodge, driven into Portage by her father to catch the next commuter flight to Toronto. Jack, who'd decided to stay at the Lodge indefinitely, barked a farewell before dashing off across the lawns.

"He loves it here." Allison smiled as she watched him go. "Even though a week ago neither of us would have believed we would choose a life in the wilderness."

"Well." Heath, standing beside her, stuck his fingers into the back pockets of his jeans and heaved a sigh. "We're on our own—you, Jack, and I."

"Yes." She turned to squint up at him in the sunlight. "Guests due in a few days, your mother not back, and this place in need of a general sprucing up. We've got our work cut out for us and no mistake. Let's get to it."

"Hang on there, boss lady." She started to move past him, but he caught her arm. "First things first. There's something I have to put right."

He took her hand to guide her into the path leading to the boathouse.

"Heath, what in the world…?"

"No words...yet." Beside the old log building he paused and looked out over the river that was gradually returning to normal after the wildness of its spring freshet. On the far side, a doe and fawn appeared out of the green freshness of the awakening forest.

The doe stared at them for a moment, then ducked her head in a sort of bow. Then she turned and bounded back into the trees, her baby at her heels.

"Heath, do you think they could be the pair we helped?" Allison breathed. "That mother seemed to acknowledge us...crazy as it seems."

"Never underestimate animals, Allie." He seized her hand. "Remember how Jack managed to find us just in the nick of time? Your grandfather had great respect for their instincts."

"And I do, too, Heath. Remember what Jack did? How he somehow knew we'd need him and ran away from the Lodge? What are you doing?" she broke off, surprised.

He was leading her to the side of the boathouse, back to the place where they'd had their first physical encounter.

"I have to make things right." He moved her carefully back against the log wall. "You can't live on the Chance haunted by a bad memory." He took her into his arms and this time, gently yet so sensuously her breath hiccupped, he kissed her. Kissed her until her senses reeled, until all she wanted was the man in her arms. "I want you to remember this only as the place I first told you I loved you," he said.

"Oh, Heath."

"What? Don't tell me I've done it wrong...again?" He drew back from her, his eyes widening.

"No, no, it's just that I didn't expect…"

"So that's not what you wanted to hear?"

"It's exactly what I wanted to hear. I didn't expect you to be so romantic about doing it."

"Sorry. I forgot. It's my wilderness man persona that turns you on." He started to take her back into his arms, but she stopped him.

"I admit you're one sexy man." She couldn't resist the tease. "But before we go any further, don't you want to hear my response?"

"If it's the right one."

"Then if the right one is that I love you, too…" She looked up to see a wicked twinkle in his eyes.

"Correct." And he was kissing her again, letting her move into position against him, letting her set the pace.

"Bad memories erased?" He pulled back and gazed into her eyes.

"Nearly." She pulled his head down to kiss him until he groaned.

"So?" His question hung in the air between them when she let him come up for air.

"So what? Are you asking me to reaffirm your ability to please lady guests?"

"Hey, cheap shot. You know what I mean. You and I. Where do we go from here?"

"Where do you want us to go?" She slanted him a sly, sideways glance.

He pulled her close to breathe the suggestion into her ear. "Into that deserted Lodge, into the nearest bedroom. But that's your decision."

"Oh, God, do you always have to be such a gentleman? Can't you just for once act the way you look?"

"What does that mean?"

"Do I have to spell it out?"

"Yeah, humor me."

"Okay, here's one for your male ego. Handsome, feral, earthy…"

"That'll do." Snatching her up so suddenly she gasped, he was striding across the grounds toward the Lodge with her in his arms before she got her breath back.

"We should discuss business first." She tried to bring her swirling senses under control. "We ought…"

"Open the door." They'd reached the Lodge and he held her in position.

"Heath…"

"Open the door, woman." He was grinning. "This wild man has waited as long as he can."

Allison Armstrong, former CFO of Shawville Industries, obeyed.

A word about the author…

Gail MacMillan is the award-winning author of twenty-six published books and numerous articles and short stories which have appeared in magazines throughout North America and western Europe.

A graduate of Queen's University, Gail lives in New Brunswick, Canada, with her husband and two dogs.